THE FIFTH CATEGORY

K. ROBERT CAMPBELL

SECOND EDITION

For more information about K. Robert Campbell, go to
authorcampbell.com

This book is dedicated to my loving
and patient wife.

Many thanks to my friend and patient
editor, Veronica Burnish.

CHAPTER ONE

The buzz; it was still there, growing louder. Cameron Scott looked up from the litter of papers on the defense counsel table and scanned the courtroom. A cold chill gripped him when he saw the source of the buzz; the judge was transforming into a man-sized hornet and rising into the air. The sound grew more piercing as Cameron stared in horror. He looked to his right in desperation, trying to see the assistant district attorney's reaction. No reaction, no assistant DA, just the cold menacing eyes of another hornet hovering over the prosecutor's table. Unable to move or speak, Cameron could only sit in cold terror as both giant hornets slowly winged toward him. The buzz was unceasing.

Cameron turned to run, but none of his limbs would function. All he could do was wait for the hornets' acid sting. As the first stab seared through his back… he awoke.

At least he thought he was awake. He felt the sweat on his face and the hard pounding of his heart, but wondered why he still heard the buzzing.

Once the fog of sleep lifted a bit he realized that the buzz of the bedside alarm had penetrated his dreams. But he still felt the stabbing pain in his back. When he rolled to his side and reached to the source of the pain, he found that he'd been lying on an ink pen. Rational thought dispelled the haze now. He remembered writing some notes about today's court hearing as he settled into bed the night before. The pen must have dropped as he dozed off.

As he reached out to punch off the alarm, Cameron wondered why his wife Mary hadn't been bothered enough by the incessant noise to cut it off herself. Ah, right, she was on a business trip.

Mary, a control room supervisor at the nearby nuclear power plant, had to attend a week-long anti-terrorist training session in Minneapolis. Cameron never slept well when she was gone; hence the late-night note-taking.

Cameron rubbed the sleep from his eyes and hoisted himself from the bed. He stumbled toward the bathroom, stopping for a moment as he saw himself in the dresser mirror. The face that stared back at him reflected his fitful night's sleep; the blue eyes sunken and hollow, the moderate paunch a bit more pronounced. He looked and felt all of his forty-five years. He knew that his usual activities kept him in better shape than he looked at the moment, so he made a mental note to curb his sweet tooth.

He turned his gaze to a framed photo of Mary on the dresser and smiled. Normally, he and Mary were not very photogenic, but this picture was one of his favorites; it depicted the mischief in her dark green eyes perfectly. Cameron found her more attractive now than he did the day they met over twenty years earlier, while he was in law school.

A glance at his nearby wristwatch told him he did not have much time for sentimental reflection so he stretched and continued to the bathroom for his morning cleanup.

A good shave and shower left Cameron feeling much more refreshed. He gathered his notes from the bed, pulled up the covers in a facsimile of bed-making, and headed downstairs. On the way to the kitchen he threw the notes into his open briefcase on a side table by the front door.

Breakfast was usually by rote; a bowl of frosted shredded wheat and a glass of orange juice. No thinking, no deciding, mind clear for planning the day. Normally by Cameron's daily breakfast-time, Mary was dressed and out of the house, since her control-room job started an hour before he went to his office. There was never an issue of having breakfast together on work days; she didn't like to eat first thing in the morning, and he didn't like to talk first thing in the morning.

Cameron's breakfast thoughts this morning were about criminal court. He had several minor cases to handle today, mostly traffic offenses that he could plea-bargain, and one felony first-appearance.

If not for the seriousness of the charges, the felony case could be considered a joke; his client had been caught literally with his hand in the cookie jar. From the police report and an interview with the deputy who filed it, Cameron learned that his client, a fisherman in Cameron's coastal hometown of Riverport, North Carolina, broke into a small country store at three in the morning. When his entry set off a silent alarm, the sheriff's dispatcher issued the alert to a patrolling deputy who was near the store.

Making a silent approach, the deputy got to the store in minutes, cutting off his lights shortly before arriving. The owner, also alerted by the alarm, met the deputy outside the store and quietly unlocked a side door for him. A lone man inside was noisily rattling something in front of him, cursing for all he was worth, and ambient light from display cases enabled the deputy to stealthily approach him from behind.

With his pistol in hand, the deputy snapped on a flashlight as he ordered the man to raise his hands. When the man hesitated for a moment, the deputy took aim and barked the order again. The man raised both hands. His left hand was empty but his right hand was stuck in a glass commercial cookie jar full of large, wrapped chocolate chip cookies. Signaling the store owner to turn on the overhead lights, the deputy told the man to turn around.

The store owner and deputy immediately recognized the thief, the deputy having arrested him before on minor misdemeanor charges and the store owner having seen him in the store on occasion. Apparently the man had no car, or maybe no license, since he usually came to the store in someone else's vehicle.

Despite his reputation as a drunk and drug user, the man generally was considered harmless. His name was Steve Raeford but he was nicknamed "Fishbait" after a wolf fish bit off his right index finger years ago when he worked on a fishing boat in Maine. Fishbait's missing finger made some tasks difficult and it was causing him trouble the night he got arrested. As Fishbait told the story, he was walking out in the country and got hungry. Nothing being open that hour of the morning, he broke in to get something to eat. After fetching a sandwich and cold drink from a lighted display case, he tried to get a cookie out of a jar with his bad hand. When the deputy caught him, he was fumbling with one of the packages and in his panic couldn't get his hand out of the jar.

When the deputy asked why he was walking on a road at least seven miles from his home at three in the morning, Fishbait answered with a shrug and mumbled something about being restless. The deputy took Fishbait before a magistrate to get his bail set and then escorted him to a cell in the county jail. Since he broke into the store with the intent to steal something, Fishbait was charged with felony breaking and entering and larceny.

When Cameron asked the arresting deputy why he entered the store without waiting for backup, the deputy explained that there were several previous incidents of neighborhood teenagers breaking into the store to steal beer. When he saw no cars nearby, he figured the same kids were at it again and felt he would not be in serious danger.

CHAPTER TWO

Even after several years of practice, Cameron had yet to remove himself from the list of attorneys appointed to indigent-criminal cases. There was no particular reason for the oversight except that he never seemed to be in the right place at the right time to mention it to anyone. In fact Cameron often used his "time/thought/opportunity convergence" excuse on Mary when chores got left undone; a chore had to come to mind when he had time to do it and nothing else held priority. Usually, Mary did not buy the excuse.

Normally, judges only assigned indigent cases to Cameron when newer attorneys were overloaded. Such was the circumstance this week, and such was the reason Cameron was reflecting on Fishbait's comedy of errors over breakfast; Fishbait had qualified for court-appointed counsel and the docket was busy enough for Cameron to enter the rotation. Although he found time to review the case the day before, Cameron's schedule was too hectic for him to talk to Fishbait at the jail. He planned to take care of that after today's first appearance, when Fishbait would enter his 'not guilty' plea.

After downing the last of his orange juice and clearing the table, Cameron headed out the door, grabbing his briefcase on the way. His office was only a few blocks from home but he rarely walked to work. The courthouse was fifteen miles away and he needed his vehicle for that trip.

Cameron just had time to say good morning to his three secretaries, new associate Ben, and receptionist Nedra, and then check his messages before heading to the courthouse. Nedra drew his attention to the top phone-message slip. The District Attorney's office called to say that there was a problem concerning his client, Mr. Raeford.

According to Nedra, the caller gave no detail, saying he would talk to Cameron in court. Cameron stuffed the slip into his pocket and left, wondering what prompted the cryptic message.

Cameron's preferred mode of travel was his pickup truck, which was not unusual for attorneys in his rural county. His Dodge Ram was a few years old and it fit him like a well-worn pair of shoes. The one alteration he made was installation of a remote ignition device that started the truck with the push of a button on his key ring. Remote ignition was not a factory option when he bought the truck, but years of car tinkering gave him the skills to install the after-market starter himself. He bought it after a particularly harsh winter, figuring he could let the truck warm up before he got in it.

Ordinarily Cameron liked a little winter, the southern kind that doesn't last too long and rarely dips below freezing, but that winter brought sub-teen temperatures and a record snowfall to Riverport. It was one of several recent weather aberrations plaguing the area lately. The past spring, Cameron witnessed six ocean waterspouts one day and dime-size hail a few days later. His town also saw a rise in hurricane activity over the last few years, both in number and intensity. Cameron, who could form a theory for just about anything, figured that a recent el Niño weather disturbance in the Pacific was adversely affecting Atlantic weather patterns.

Experts predicted twenty-five tropical storms for the current hurricane season, fourteen of which might reach hurricane strength. By the end of July, twelve tropical storms had formed, three of which became hurricanes of category two or less. Two of the hurricanes never reached land, and the remaining one exhausted itself to tropical storm level by the time it reached Florida. It was now August, and as he listened to the radio on the way to the courthouse, Cameron heard a meteorologist warn that tropical depression thirteen was forming off the west coast of Africa. He made a mental note to pick up a supply of fresh batteries on the way home.

At the courthouse Cameron picked his way through the maze of hall-dwellers waiting for court to convene, and headed into the downstairs courtroom where traffic cases, misdemeanors, and first-appearances were heard. Assistant district attorney Bill Lutz was at the prosecutor's table talking to some people with pink traffic citations in their hands, presumably asking to have their charges reduced or their cases put off. Moving within Lutz's line of sight, Cameron held up the telephone-message slip he got from Nedra.

Eventually Lutz looked up, nodded acknowledgment that the message was his, and abruptly turned back to the business at hand. To Cameron, Lutz looked nervous.

After a minute or two, Lutz finished talking to the pink-slip people and Cameron hurried over to speak with him before anyone else came up. "I got your message about Fishbait" said Cameron, "but it didn't really tell me much."

Lutz hesitated for a moment before responding, seeming to grope for the right words. Finally, he said "Yeah, well, there's been a problem in the jail."

"What kind of problem?"

"Your client didn't get up this morning."

"What, the jailers are allowing sleep-ins now?"

"Let me put it this way Scotty, your client won't be getting up at all."

Cameron's face flushed as he drew closer to Lutz and said, "What the hell's the matter with you, Bill? You know I hate that nickname. I never should have told you about it when we were in law school."

Looking flustered, Lutz answered, "I know, I'm sorry. I'm just.... Anyway, about your client...."

Cameron could tell something was troubling Lutz, but he had more pressing issues and asked, "Are you telling me my client is dead?"

"That's what I'm telling you."

"What happened?"

"We don't know. He fell violently ill in the TV room last night during prisoner recreation time. By the time they got him to the hospital, he was dead."

"Was an autopsy done?"

"None was ordered and I doubt one will be done."

Noting that Bill was avoiding eye contact, Cameron pressed on, "You mean to tell me a man in the sheriff's custody died of unknown causes and no one bothered to investigate? That doesn't make sense."

"I guess everyone figured he OD'd or something. Look, you know he's a doper. Maybe somebody smuggled bad stuff to him in the jail. He sure won't be making a first appearance now, so why don't you just forget him. You know the State will still pay you for the time you've put in."

"What's gotten into you Bill? I can't believe you're ignoring standard procedure. You know damn well your office is supposed to investigate jail deaths, especially if drugs are involved."

11

Lutz folded his arms and made no response. Cameron shook his head and continued, "Look Bill, I know Fishbait's a doper, but he's been clean for several months now. I see his sister Raylene a lot at the restaurant where she works, and she's been bragging on him."

Cameron also knew that Fishbait's sister was his only surviving relative in the state. Although close to forty, she had never married. Instead she devoted her life to her brother, trying her best to keep him clean, sober, and working. They shared a house in Riverport and Raylene's work at the restaurant kept them fed and sheltered. She was well liked by her customers, but seldom socialized.

Lutz opened his mouth as if to say something but shrugged instead. Cameron countered, "What the hell's gotten into you? Ever since we were study partners in law school I've known you to be a stickler for the rules."

Lutz's tone grew edgier, "All right Cameron, don't push it. The DA says there's nothing there to look into and he has the authority to investigate or let it go. I'm just an assistant. End of story. You got any other cases today? I've got people lined up."

Frustrated, but seeing futility in pursuing the matter further, Cameron arranged the traffic pleas for his remaining clients with Bill and entered them once court was in session. But the nightmare from which he awoke just hours earlier kept creeping into his thoughts.

After taking care of some other matters in the register of deeds and clerk's offices, and grabbing lunch at the courthouse cafeteria, Cameron headed back to the office for the afternoon.

CHAPTER THREE

Cameron conducted a real estate closing and checked the day's mail before turning to the pile of messages that Nedra had handed him on his way past the front desk. Most were routine but one caught his eye immediately. It was from Fishbait's sister Raylene Raeford, who called while Cameron was at the courthouse. Nedra noted on the message that Raylene would be home all day. When Cameron called, she picked up on the first ring.

"Raylene, this is Cameron Scott. I just got back in from the courthouse. I heard about your brother and I'm very sorry. Is there anything I can do for you?"

"Thanks so much for calling right away, Mr. Scott." Raylene always called him the formal 'Mr. Scott', even when waiting his table at the restaurant. "I didn't know where else to turn. I probably should be crying my eyes out now, but I'm kind of in shock. Anyway, I'm not sure what to do with all of Steven's things, especially the money."

"Well, first you need to call the funeral home where they took him and make arrangements with them for his burial, or whatever."

"I guess it's too late for that, he's already been cremated."

"He's been what?"

"You know, cremated. He's already ashes."

"Did you authorize that?"

"No. I asked the deputy that first called me where they took Steven and she told me it was already 'taken care of'. She said the funeral home would bring his ashes to me in some kind of container."

Cameron paused for a moment, amazed at the additional rule violations, then answered, "As his closest kin, you should have been the one to authorize a cremation, but we'll come back to that. You'll

13

need to apply to the clerk to be his estate administrator, assuming he had no will. I'll help you with the preliminary paperwork, but the rest should be pretty easy, since I don't think he had very much, did he?" Cameron assumed that Fishbait and Raylene lived hand-to-mouth, doubting that Fishbait spent the money to have a will drawn.

"You're right about the will, but not the rest. You see, Steven had ten thousand dollars cash money stuck away in his dresser drawer. I'm off today, and was catching up on some laundry before the deputy called…"

"Wait a minute; they didn't call you until this morning? I thought he went to the hospital last night."

"The first I knew about it was this morning about nine o'clock. I just figured he spent another night out with some of his friends, like he sometimes does… did." She took a moment to regain her composure. "Anyway, as I was putting away some of his socks, I noticed the bundle of hundreds. It was just kind of stuffed in the drawer, not like he was really trying to hide it. I know it wasn't there three days ago, because I'd put some clean socks in the same drawer then."

Cameron wondered if Fishbait had gone from using drugs to dealing, although he could not imagine Fishbait surviving in that atmosphere for long. He asked Raylene, "Are you sure Fishbait… I mean Steven… has been clean? You haven't found any more drugs in any of his stuff?"

"I haven't found anything, and he knows I check to be sure he doesn't bring any of it into the house. That's the last thing I need is for him to get me busted."

"…and he hadn't shown any signs that he was using?"

"Nothing. I know how he gets when he's doping, and he just didn't have any of the signs. In fact, I told him just the other day how proud I was that he was staying clean. He even spent last weekend trying to fix some of the bricks and blocks that come loose on the barbecue pit out back of the house. Bless his heart, he wasn't very good at it."

"He hasn't been hanging around with anyone suspicious that you know of?"

"Not that I know of, but I've been working and don't know who he might have seen during the day for the last couple of weeks. But I'd think that if he was dealing he wouldn't trust any place to put the stuff but home, and I know he wasn't keeping anything here. Like I said, I keep a pretty good check on things when I clean up, and there's not many hiding places here."

"Hmm. That's pretty strange. Listen, did he show any signs of bad health lately?"

"No. In fact I sent him to the clinic a couple weeks ago for a checkup, to see how his health was holding up once he went clean. They said he hadn't done himself any serious damage yet, and he should try to keep it that way. That might be some of what kept him off the stuff up to now."

"So you don't have any idea of what might have… done him in?"

"No, but I wish you'd look into it. I'm getting over the shock some now and I'm just starting to get mad at how it was handled. You think you can find anything out?"

"I'll do what I can. You take care, and let me know if anything else comes up. I'll try to get over to the jail tomorrow and ask some questions. Meantime, find the safest place you can for that cash and let me know right away if anyone asks about it. When you mentioned not knowing what to do with his money a while ago I thought you meant his last paycheck or something. Hold off putting it in the bank though; something tells me it might not be his."

"I will. And thanks, Mr. Scott. I don't have a whole lot to pay you, but…"

"Don't worry; just pay what you can when you can."

"Well, I appreciate that. You know how things have been."

"I understand. I'll try to hold the billings to a minimum. Take care." Cameron's mind was racing as he slid the phone receiver onto its cradle. The "Cookie Caper" was becoming more bizarre at every turn. Fishbait, in jail for something that would have pled out as a misdemeanor, dies for no apparent reason. The Sheriff and DA's office ignore procedure and order no autopsy and then hurry to have him cremated, somehow bypassing procedure on that, too. Then his sister finds a wad of cash stashed in a sock drawer with no explanation for its presence. Cameron wondered if the authorities were aware of the cash yet, although he doubted it.

CHAPTER FOUR

The next morning, Cameron had several matters to handle in the office before he could get to the courthouse complex and he arrived there just after lunchtime. He knew all the jailers pretty well, especially Elliott Grainger, the one who had been on duty the night before. Elliott was a likable twenty-five year old, tall and lanky with short black hair and as much mustache as the sheriff would allow his men to grow.

Cameron remembered when Elliott's father, a Riverport policeman, was killed in service soon after Elliott turned fifteen. The city paid Mrs. Grainger a modest widow's pension but it fell on Elliott, the oldest of five children, to take after-school jobs for the family to survive.

Cameron provided some of that work, hiring him to clean the office once a week. He also took Elliott under his wing, serving more as a big brother than a father-figure and helping him through some rough times over the loss of his dad.

Elliott finished high school on his mother's and Cameron's insistence, then hired on as a deputy sheriff as soon as he could finish basic law enforcement training. He married at twenty but still helped his mother with the expense of raising his brothers and sisters by working extra shifts as a jailer. A few weeks ago, he told Cameron that his youngest sibling was nearing high school graduation, so he planned to cut back on the overtime. His goal now was to further his education and make his way to detective.

Cameron also recalled that at age twenty-one, Elliott had been arrested in a neighboring county for drunk driving, a charge that could have cost him his law-enforcement career. Having consumed only one beer while visiting a friend, not near enough to warrant the charges, he turned to Cameron for legal help.

Cameron's investigation established that the arresting officer had not properly maintained the Breathalyzer, which caused it to give a false reading. As a result, the prosecutor dismissed the charge before trial. Not only did Elliott keep his job, but Cameron had refused to bill him for his services. A grateful Elliott told Cameron that he was indebted to him and Cameron joked about getting a return of the favor some day, though he never expected a repayment. It now looked like he needed to take Elliott up on the offer after all.

It was nearly two o'clock by the time Cameron could get to the jailhouse and Elliott was already back on duty. After exchanging some small talk with Elliott, Cameron brought up the subject of the previous evening's events.

"Elliott, I think I may need to call in that favor we always talk about" he said bluntly, "and I'll do it by asking you to help me figure out a little bit about what happened in here the other night. Evidently, there's no ongoing investigation—in fact, there's been no investigation at all as far as I can tell—so there shouldn't be any problem in your answering a few questions. You just tell me if you start to feel too uncomfortable about it, OK?"

"Sure, but if it's about Fishbait dying here, who's your client?"

"Fair enough. I can tell you it's his sister. She's a little upset about not being notified."

"Well I don't understand that. She's the one who told EMS to take him straight on over to the funeral home and don't bother with an autopsy."

Cameron tried not to register his surprise. "Did you talk to her?"

"Well, no, I didn't talk to her direct, but that's what I was told."

"Who told you?"

Elliott hesitated, then said, "You told me to tell you if I felt uncomfortable, and I'm not sure if I should get anybody else into this."

"That's all right; it's not important. Just tell me what you feel you can."

Elliott took a moment to collect his thoughts. "It was about eight o'clock, and the prisoners were in the TV room. The low-risk ones are allowed to go in and have a smoke and watch television from about seven to nine each night. The Sheriff doesn't let them smoke anywhere else but there and the exercise yard, where there's not much that would catch fire very easy. Sometimes if there's two of us on duty I'll go down and watch a show with them and smoke one of my own. If not, I have to lock them in and keep track on the monitor."

"Was Fishbait smoking?"

"He sure was."

"Where do they usually keep their cigarettes?"

"We keep them at the desk. If they had any when they're brought in, or if anybody brings them some, we stick a name label on them, and pass the packs out at the TV room. That's where Fishbait was when we gave him his pack."

"So, Fishbait had some cigarettes on him when he got picked up?"

"Well now that you mention it, no. His sister brought him some; or at least I guess it was his sister."

"Why do you say that?"

"Well, I never really saw her; one of the new morning jailers did. She told me a lady showed up during morning shift saying she was his sister and that she wanted him to have his cigarettes and some candy bars, too. It wasn't visiting hours, so they ran it all through x-ray to be sure nothing was hidden inside, labeled it all for him, and told him it was there. He seemed a little surprised that she brought the cigarettes. He said she didn't usually like him smoking but guessed it was because he was in the jail and she felt sorry."

Cameron thought it curious that Raylene had not mentioned her visit to the jail, and made a mental note to question her about it. "OK, what happened in the TV room?"

"I left Wagoner, the other jailer, back at the desk and went down to the TV room to watch over things there. I'd passed out everybody's cigarettes and they were watching some comedy show while they smoked. Fishbait had just lit up when he all of a sudden started choking and rolled over sideways. I couldn't do a whole lot right away, because we have to get everybody back in their cells if something unusual happens."

"And how did you get them all out?"

"I called on the intercom for Wagoner to bring some trustees to help get everybody back. There weren't but five prisoners in there to begin with, so that didn't take long. Meantime, I could see that Fishbait was starting to turn blue, so I called the 911 center direct on my radio. Before I could do much more, he was a goner. By that time, I wasn't feeling too good my self for some reason."

"How long did it take the medics to get there?"

"Only a couple minutes. They were there by the time Wagoner got everybody cleared out of the room. Fishbait's sister left a cell-phone number when she brought the cigarettes so Wagoner called to tell her that her brother was on the way to the hospital. The EMT's told me he was already dead, but we didn't tell her that."

"Why not?"

"We're supposed to let the doctors do that, since none of us were qualified to pronounce him dead."

"That makes sense. What happened to his belongings?"

"Wagoner said we should send them out with the rescue people because Fishbait wouldn't be coming back. I told him since he was almost off duty, he might as well go to the hospital in case they needed more information. I was feeling better by then after rescue gave me some oxygen. Wagoner wanted me to go and him stay and straighten up the TV room, but I told him I was senior officer on duty and would have to be the one to stay. I also told him I'd take care of the TV room. He wanted to argue, but I told him to go on."

"The cigarettes went with the rescue crew then?"

"Either that or Wagoner took them with him. I really didn't pay that much attention to where they went, but I know we don't still have them. Even if they got thrown away, we empty the trash every day so they're probably at the landfill by now. How come you're so interested in those?"

"Oh, just trying to check everything out." Cameron actually was trying to decide if the cigarettes had caused Fishbait to choke up somehow, but did not want the jailer to know where he was headed with the inquiry. "Did he eat any of the candy?"

"No, he never got a chance to. We sent that on with his other things that were still at the front desk."

Cameron concluded the interview. "Listen, Elliott, I appreciate you answering my questions, and I have one more small favor to ask, and then I'll consider us even. I'd like to go down and check out the TV room."

"I'm not supposed to let anybody but the prisoners and jail personnel down there, but I do owe you big time. Just don't tell nobody I let you in. Or if anybody sees you, tell them you took a wrong turn."

Trying to ease Elliott's nervousness, Cameron grinned as he responded: "I just hope they won't try to keep me."

19

Elliott pressed the buttons for the electronic locks, and waved Cameron on to the now-empty TV room. Cameron gingerly made his way down the hall, uncertain of where he was going or what he was going to do.

CHAPTER FIVE

Cameron was not sure what he wanted to look for in the TV room. He was still trying to digest the new information Elliott had divulged, especially the revelation that Raylene actually knew that night about Fishbait's death and apparently authorized his cremation. He could not understand why she would lie about that and then send him on a mission that would uncover the truth. But then, Elliott said he had not seen Raylene and thus would not know if it really was her. Did Fishbait have a girlfriend that Raylene was not aware of? And if so, why would she pretend to be his sister?

As he entered the TV room, Cameron put the lingering questions aside and turned his thoughts to inspecting the room. There was not much to take in. The television was firmly attached to a steel table, which was firmly attached to one wall of the room.

There were three rows of five heavy plastic seats facing the television, each bolted to the floor. Molded into the arm of each seat was a depression that served as an ashtray. Steel benches were attached to two walls, meeting at a steel table in the corner. The table also had indentations that served as ashtrays. The overall impression was of a room that contained nothing that could be thrown or taken out, and it obviously had been cleaned that morning, since the ashtrays were all empty.

Looking up the painted cinderblock walls toward the ceiling, Cameron could see two small surveillance cameras on opposite corners and surmised they had wide-angle lenses that could sweep the entire room at one time. He avoided looking directly into either one. Next to the entry door there was an intercom with a push button. Cameron walked over to it and pressed. As he expected, Elliott's voice sounded from the intercom speaker: "Yes, are you ready to come out now?"

"Not quite yet, Elliott. Do you recall where Fishbait was sitting when he started to choke?"

"Yessir, right over on the metal bench, at the wall opposite where you are. I was on that other bench." Cameron realized that Elliott, ever the diligent jailer, was watching him on the surveillance screen.

"Thanks Elliott, I'll buzz again when I'm ready to come out."

There was no response, so Cameron began looking around the room again. He still did not know what he was looking for, but hoped something would present itself. While that hope remained in his mind, his gaze dropped to the floor below the bench that Elliott had mentioned. He leaned down a bit so that he could see the back wall under the bench.

Bingo. There unnoticed by whichever trustees had been sweeping the last two days was a cigarette butt, in the juncture of wall and floor. It was not much, but in the otherwise sterile room, it offered some possible information. Cameron sensed that Elliott was still monitoring his movements within the room. He needed a diversion to mask his actions when he retrieved the only bit of evidence he had found. Realizing he had his hand-held dictation recorder in his pocket, he took it out and began speaking into it. As he strolled toward the bench, still feigning dictation, he let the recorder slip from his hand. As he had hoped, the battery compartment opened on impact, and recorder, battery cover, and batteries scattered in different directions, one battery rolling under the bench.

Slumping his shoulders and trying to give his best impersonation of an embarrassed klutz, Cameron leaned down and began picking up the scattered pieces. When he came to the errant battery under the bench, he did his best to block the camera view with his body as he scooped up battery and cigarette butt at one time. Shaking his head, still in mock embarrassment, he quickly slid all the pieces into his pocket, walked over to the intercom and pressed the button.

Elliott was laughing as Cameron approached the front desk to make his exit. "Boy, I'm glad you didn't get that clumsy when you were handling my case."

Cameron faked a quizzical look, saying, "I'm not sure I follow you."

"I was watching you on the TV screen here. You had to have seen the cameras in there."

Now trying to look sheepish, Cameron replied "Ohmygosh, I did see them, but I didn't know I had an audience while I was in there."

"I didn't mean to embarrass you, but it was funny. Anyway, I still have to do my job here, so I'm sorry I had to keep an eye on you."

"I understand. I guess I should have expected it," Cameron laughed. "Now my face is red." It was red, but more from the exertion of leaning under the bench than from embarrassment.

CHAPTER SIX

Cameron went straight back to the office, waded through paperwork and caught up on telephone calls, then went home and ate a quick supper. Today was the last day of Mary's seminar and she was supposed to fly home in the morning. He missed her and never felt quite right when she was not there. He waited long enough for her to eat and get back to her room before calling and she picked up on the second ring, saying "Love you, miss you."

He responded, laughing, "How do you know who you're loving and missing? It could have been the front desk."

"Nah, I could tell it was you by the way the phone rang."

"If you've become that much of a clairvoyant, I should curb my dirty thoughts. I miss you, too."

They settled into a couple's conversation, catching each other up on the day's activities. She'd been learning how to spot irregular behavior in her co-workers that could indicate involvement in terrorist activities.

"Oh, great," he said, "our lights will be going out because everyone at the power plant is too busy watching each other instead of the controls."

She laughed, and he told her that most of his day had been pretty ordinary, except for one developing case. Mary knew that he could not give her much detail without revealing confidential information. She had to settle for a general recital about a prisoner who had died under odd circumstances and the fact that Cameron had been "retained" to look into those circumstances.

Toward the end of the conversation, Mary told Cameron that he should watch the news tonight and see what was happening in the tropics. The television news she had seen at the hotel that morning gave passing mention of a developing storm, but without the detail their home station would give. Cameron knew that Mary's schedule the night before included a dinner and late classes. As a result, he had foregone calling her and did his paperwork with the television off, so he was unaware of the storm warnings. He promised her that he would watch the news tonight, and they said their goodbyes. Her mention of the storm reminded him that he had forgotten to buy batteries on the way home and he promised himself that he would pick them up tomorrow.

Cameron tried to relax by watching a few comedy shows on television, hoping Elliott hadn't seen through his little comedy earlier in the day. He had sealed the cigarette butt in a plastic bag, planning to take it to a chemist friend on his way to the airport to pick up Mary the next morning.

Finally, the evening news came on. The local news emanated from Whittington, a port city about twenty miles north of Riverport, and the only city in that part of the state large enough to support television stations. Not much newsworthy had happened in Whittington that day, and Cameron wondered why no mention was made of the jail death in its neighboring county. He guessed that poor Fishbait did not even rate a passing mention.

Shortly, the weather report began. Cameron was surprised to learn that not only had the tropical depression off of Africa strengthened to a tropical storm overnight, but two more depressions were forming in the Caribbean.

The new tropical storm, number thirteen, had been given the name "Mary". "*So that's really why she wanted me to watch the weather*" thought Cameron. "*If this one packs the energy of my Mary, we're in for trouble.*"

CHAPTER SEVEN

At seven the next morning, Cameron started the forty-five minute drive north to the airport, just past Whittington. Mary's flight was not due until nine forty-five, giving him time to see his chemist friend in Palmwood, a bedroom community along the route.

The chemist was Wally Johnson, who worked for a nearby supplier of chemical compounds used in the textile industry. He and Cameron had known each other for at least fifteen years, after meeting at a model train show and discovering a mutual interest in O-gauge railroading. They had helped each other build detailed train layouts and met on sporadic Saturdays for operating sessions.

During those train-operating sessions, Cameron learned that in addition to overseeing quality control for the product of the chemical plant, Wally was charged with developing and testing new chemical compounds. According to Wally, the plant's laboratory was state-of-the-art and he was subject to little supervision in its use.

Wally was expecting Cameron. The night before, Cameron had called, saying, "Wally, I've got to pick Mary up at the airport tomorrow morning. I wonder if I might drop by around seven-thirty or so to show you some new layout plans."

Wally answered, "Sure, I'll have a few minutes before I have to leave for work. You tired of your old track plan?"

"Nah, just some minor track changes."

"Okay, see you in the morning."

When Cameron arrived, Wally answered the door immediately and invited him into the living room. They settled into their chairs and Wally asked, "Want some coffee or something?"

Cameron answered, "Oh, no thanks, I had some before I left the house."

Wally looked at this watch and said, "I guess we'd better go over those plans then. Are you thinking of adding some of that flexible track?"

Cameron responded, "Actually, I have something else I really need to show you," and handed him the plastic bag with the cigarette butt inside. He then added, "I wonder if you might be able to give this a chemical analysis. I wasn't sure how I was going to explain this over the phone, so I hope you forgive the subterfuge.".

"Other than the tar and nicotine content, is there anything in particular you're looking for?" Wally asked.

Cameron answered, "I'm not really sure, but I think this cigarette may have caused a man's death."

"That usually takes several cigarettes a day for several years. Why this one cigarette?"

"Oh, just one of my hunches. I think it's got a little more than the usual flavor enhancers in it. I can't go into a lot of detail yet, but I'd appreciate it if you'd see what you can find out."

Wally laughed and said, "Well, I'm certainly not going to challenge one of your hunches again."

The one time Wally had challenged him about a hunch, Cameron took a half-hour to detail the thought patterns that only took a few seconds for his mind to process. Drawing on bits and pieces of knowledge he had gained over the years, combining them with the facts at hand, and adding a touch of intuition, Cameron often formulated an answer to a problem before most people knew there was a problem.

"All right", said Wally, "I've got a pretty busy day today, but I'll try to fit it in. I'll call when I get some results. Should I call your office?"

Cameron stood and said, "That'll be good, but if you can't get me directly just leave a message to call back, with no other detail."

As Wally walked Cameron to the door, he said, "I understand. But you do know you owe me some railroad plans now."

They laughed and shook hands, and Cameron continued his journey to the airport. As he reentered the main road to Whittington, Cameron noticed a car parked on the roadside with a man inside reading a roadmap. Something about the car looked familiar, but Cameron figured that it was because it looked like a standard-issue government sedan; no frills, ugly paint, and plain cloth upholstery, with a no-frills, poorly dressed occupant.

He also noticed that the sedan had Virginia tags, although they were not government-issue.

After rounding a curve and traveling another half mile, Cameron glanced at his rearview mirror and noticed that the same sedan was traveling several hundred yards behind him. Figuring the man had found his bearings on the map, he turned his attention to the buttons on the car radio, looking for a station that was not all commercials. Soon, the other car and driver were forgotten. He followed the usual route to the airport and was there in a short time.

He took his parking permit from a machine and found a spot surprisingly close to the terminal, locked the truck and headed for the main door. As he reached the glass-walled entryway into the terminal, an odd reflection caught his eye; he could see the Virginia sedan slowly passing behind his truck in the parking lot.

CHAPTER EIGHT

Cameron checked his watch as he entered the airport lobby and saw that he had only a fifteen minute wait until Mary's plane was due. The information board in the lobby indicated that her flight was on time. Since he had skipped breakfast in his hurry to see Wally, he bought a honey bun and small bottle of orange juice from a vendor in the waiting area. Non-passengers were not permitted into the gate areas, so he settled into a seat in the lobby where he could see Mary as she came to the main concourse. He began eating as he read a Whittington newspaper that had been left on the seat.

The newspaper had no report of Fishbait's death, but there was much front-page coverage about increased levels of terrorist threats on unnamed U.S. targets. Cameron was glad Mary was about to be safe on the ground. He briefly worried over her work in the nuclear plant—a seemingly prime terrorist target—but knew that she probably was safer inside the plant than he would be in his office, considering the redundant safety devices and protective encasements built into the plant.

About the time Cameron reached the comics section, the lobby started bristling with activity and people rushed toward the concourse gates to greet incoming passengers. Glancing at the wall clock, Cameron knew several minutes would pass before the plane settled in enough for passengers to disembark, so he stayed seated. As he began looking back down at the comics, he suddenly got an uneasy feeling that someone was looking at him.

Lifting his eyes but not his head, Cameron scanned the area from which he felt he was being watched. No one seemed to be looking directly at him, but one man did turn his face rather suddenly, just enough so Cameron could not see his features. The man's wool tweed sports jacket with leather patches at the elbows looked familiar though, as did his tousled gray hair. The man reading his roadmap in the Virginia sedan wore the same jacket. He had his left arm propped on the window frame and the elbow patch was evident. At that time, Cameron had wondered why the man was wearing such a hot, outdated jacket during a sultry southern August.

Soon, passengers began hustling down the concourse toward the gate, so Cameron folded his paper and walked over to join the throng of greeters. Shortly he saw Mary's dark curly hair bobbing up and down among the sea of passengers. When she got closer, he waved his paper to catch her eye. She caught sight of him, smiled broadly and quickened her pace. After maneuvering through the bottleneck of people coming through the gate, she ran over to Cameron with open arms. He was doing the same, and they nearly bowled each other over as they met and embraced.

With Cameron's arms tightly locked around her, Mary was barely able to take in enough breath to tell him how much she had missed him. He responded with a kiss and a tighter squeeze that knocked the rest of the breath out of her, then quickly let go and held her out for inspection.

For a few seconds, all he could do was look in her eyes and grin. Finally he said, "Every time you go off, you come back looking more gorgeous than you did when you left," to which she replied, "I'd feel complimented if I didn't know you were just horny, you old goat." At that, he gave her a playful whack on the backside, and she said "Mr. Scott, what will your clients say?"

"They'll say, 'Awwright Mr. Scott, go for it.'"

"I wasn't thinking about your juvenile clients."

"Neither was I."

During the ensuing banter, they made their way to the baggage area and retrieved her suitcases. As they neared the glass-walled exit area, Cameron was startled once again by a reflection. He was certain that Mr. Tweedjacket was leaning on a lobby wall behind them reading his map again, trying to look inconspicuous.

Cameron laid a hand on Mary's shoulder and said, "I just saw a client I've been playing phone tag with. I'm going to go over and give him a quick message. I'll be right back.". He set the suitcases down and walked toward the man.

In case he had seen the man so many times by sheer coincidence, Cameron opted for a friendly approach, smiling as he strode quickly to the man. The man did not raise his head, but appeared to tense up as Cameron drew near. Cameron stepped directly in front of him, saying, "You don't look like you're from here and you look a little lost. Can I help you find your way somewhere?"

With a nervous chuckle, the man replied "No thanks, I think I can find my way from here."

Cameron continued, "I was worried about you because I'm sure you're the guy I passed on my way up here and you were reading a map then, too. Were you thinking there might be another airport nearby or..."

The man sighed and cut him short, "All right, you caught me. My surveillance skills are a little rusty." Producing a badge and identification card, he continued, "I'm Special Agent Gene Peterson, with the FBI and yes, I've been following you."

Cameron replied, "I guess you already know who I am, but I will ask why in the world you want to follow me? I don't think I've done anything to merit this much attention."

"You haven't, but your client has."

"I've got quite a few clients, but none who have broken any Federal laws that I know of. Do you mind telling me who?"

"Let's just say it's a client you really shouldn't worry about anymore."

"Fishbait?"

Peterson looked surprised. "Who?"

"Sorry, I figured you'd know his nickname. Steven Raeford. He was known locally as 'Fishbait.'"

"I haven't been down here long enough to learn any nicknames, but yes, your 'Fishbait' is who we're talking about."

Cameron looked toward Mary and said, "Agent Peterson, I'd like to get my wife home, but you've made me curious. How about coming by my office about eleven tomorrow so we can continue the conversation? We're closed on Saturdays, so nobody else will be there."

"That'll work out fine. I was planning to talk to you after today's surveillance."

"Yeah, you might want to brush up on your skills there."

"I usually don't follow people. I'll have to learn to blend in better. What tipped you off?"

"The jacket. And the car. You might want to invest in a short-sleeve plaid shirt and rent a pickup truck for starters." Another nervous laugh from Peterson.

"Just kidding, but you really do need to dump the tweed jacket if you're going to do outside surveillance in this heat." Cameron gave Peterson directions to his office, gave him a mock salute, and returned to Mary.

Mary and Cameron made small talk for a few minutes as they walked to the truck, then Mary asked, "Why were you really talking to that man?"

Surmising that she had seen Peterson show his identification, Cameron answered, "I'm sorry about the little fib, but I wasn't sure who the guy was. Seemed like he was stalking me a good part of the day, and I wanted to find out what he was really up to. Turned out he's an FBI agent, and he's interested in my dead client."

"He didn't say why?" Cameron was throwing Mary's suitcases into the back seat of the truck but he saw a worried look pass across her face.

"I didn't give him a chance to. I was anxious to get you home, and I'd rather talk to him on my own turf anyway. He's coming to the office tomorrow."

"Or so he says."

"I think he'll show up. I know who he is now, and I suspect he's got something he wants to tell me anyway. He looks like a career man. You'd think they'd give him a better assignment than following a country lawyer around."

"Well, just be careful."

"You know I will. I'll let you know if anything serious comes out of it. In the meantime, tell me what you learned in Minneapolis."

Mary did not seem quite satisfied with his answer, but took the hint that he wanted the subject dropped. She began telling him about the terrorism seminar as they climbed into the truck and started home. After hearing some of what she had learned, Cameron could understand her concern about the FBI's involvement in his case.

As they traveled homeward, the discussion turned to more mundane—and more comfortable—subject matters. They spent the rest of the day at home, and caught up on other things that night.

CHAPTER NINE

Cameron walked to his office building the next morning and when he got there at eleven, Agent Peterson was already parked in front. Nedra's car was there as well, and Cameron surmised that she must be using the quiet weekend time to catch up on some filing.

After escorting Peterson to a seat in his personal office, Cameron closed the door and settled into his own desk chair. He got right to the point, "All right Special Agent Peterson, would you please tell me why you would want to spend your time chasing me around the county?"

Peterson also got right to the point. "Mr. Scott, we believe your client, Mr. Raeford, got himself involved with a major drug cartel and was seriously in over his head. We know he had been given a sizable amount of cash at some point in the last few days, and we think he was on his way to pick up a shipment when he made his little side trip to the store and got caught."

"That doesn't add up," interjected Cameron, "From what I've been told, he didn't have any cash on him, and he was on foot."

"I'm well aware of that. The cash was a down-payment on the work he was to do. According to my informants, he was to walk to a meeting point, where he would pick up a car with drugs hidden in it, along with a note telling him where to drive it. We think the destination was somewhere in New York or New Jersey. Someone at the destination point would hand him an envelope with the balance of his payment in cash, then he'd take a cab to the nearest airport and use some of the cash to fly back home. His was a small but important link in the transportation route for the drugs. Evidently, they planned to use him more than once."

"So the drugs weren't meant for local consumption."

"Hardly. The street value would be in the millions. The drugs start in Columbia, and come into the U.S. through Mexico at the Texas border. Your county seems to be the midway link in a perverted type of Underground Railroad."

Although he already doubted much of Peterson's explanation, Cameron said, "Makes sense so far, but you haven't explained why you needed to follow me."

"Believe it or not, we originally had better surveillance in place on your client. Our local agents were hoping he would lead us to the pickup point, but he short-circuited their plans with his little stopover. He was in the jail before they could intervene. They stayed near, thinking he would be released the next day and would try to finish his journey."

"But they didn't count on Fishbait not making bail. Why didn't your people just arrange to have him sprung anyway?"

"That's the sticky part. The Sheriff didn't know we were here."

"Why would you not tell him? Don't tell me you think he's involved in this mess, because I wouldn't believe you if you did. I've known Sheriff Hiles for years and…"

"Don't get yourself all worked up for nothing. Nobody thinks he's involved, but we do think one of his deputies is on the take. The trouble is, we can't pinpoint who it is and we didn't want to tip them off that we're looking. You don't have to worry about keeping this a secret from the Sheriff though, because we met with him yesterday afternoon. I can't say he's happy with us, but he's cooperating with the investigation."

"OK, so when do we get to the reason you were tailing me?"

"I was called in after your client's unexpected demise. I'm in charge of the national investigation and usually stay in D.C., but this link has been the closest we've come to breaking into the supply chain. We were watching to see if you might also be involved in some way. I heard you had a lot of questions about what happened to your client and you were mighty intent on heading to the north end of the county early this morning. Of course, now I know you were headed to the airport to pick up your wife."

"But you know about my interview with Deputy Grainger yesterday?"

"I've been told you went to the jail and spoke to him, and that you spent some time looking around in the rec-room. We haven't asked the deputy about your conversation because we still don't know who's the mole in the Sheriff's office. By the way, my fellow agents are more used to field work than I am. I bet you didn't know you were being followed until I botched it, did you?"

"That's true. Do you still think I might be involved? I can tell you that Fishbait never had a chance to tell me anything, because I never got to talk to him before he died."

"We know that now, but I still would like to know what you asked Grainger and what your stop on the way to the airport was about."

"As far as my conversation with deputy Grainger, I was retained to find out what really happened to Fishbait and only asked the deputy's permission to do a little surveillance of my own. I didn't find out much, though." Cameron had a hunch that this was not the time to mention the cigarette. And now, knowing he was being tailed, he wondered how secure his phones were.

Cameron continued, "And as for my stopover, I was visiting a fellow model railroader. I'm guessing that you don't know about all my hobbies yet." The dig eliciting no response from Peterson, he went on, "I wanted to check out a scene he'd added to his pike and I thought I'd catch him before he left for work, since I was headed past his house anyway." The statement was true in parts. Wally had wanted Cameron to look at a new scene he had built, and Cameron had wanted to catch Wally before he left for work. The two things just did not happen to coincide on this trip.

"Fair enough," said Peterson. "We're going to talk to Mr. Raeford's sister today and see if he told her anything that might help. I won't ask you to divulge who wanted you to follow up on his death, but I'm assuming it was her. We've also got a pretty good idea that his down payment is somewhere in the house, and we'll need to recover that."

Cameron made a mental note to call Raylene and advise her to release the money to Peterson. He also wanted to confirm his suspicion that she was not the one who had brought the cigarettes to the jail and authorized the cremation. Still following his hunch that he should not tell Peterson any more than he was asked, he said, "OK, if there is anything else I can do to help…." He stood and hoped that Peterson would follow suit.

Peterson took the hint. He stood and shook Cameron's outstretched hand, saying, "We know how to find you. In the meantime, I think it would be best for you to drop out of this case. There's nothing more you can do for your ex-client."

Cameron escorted Peterson to his car and, after Peterson drove away, took a few moments to reflect on the conversation. Peterson had left him with more questions than answers.

As Cameron pondered, Nedra hurried outside to meet him and handed him a message slip, saying, "I didn't know you'd be leaving so soon. Your friend Wally called earlier this morning and said it was urgent. Who just left?"

Cameron replied, "Oh, some FBI agent looking into a case. When did Wally call?"

Nedra responded, "About eight thirty. He said he got the answer you wanted, whatever that means."

Seeing that Nedra was carrying her pocketbook, Cameron said, "Do you mind if I borrow your cell phone? I can just call him from here." Nedra fished out her phone and handed it to him, saying, "I've got to finish locking up. I'll be right back."

After Nedra went back inside, Cameron eagerly dialed the number shown on the message. First confirming that Wally was using someone else's cell phone as well, Cameron asked, "Did you find out anything useful?"

Wally replied, "Yes and the results of my lab analysis are disturbing: The extra ingredient in that cigarette was cyanide, concentrated enough to kill on the first drag."

Cameron thought, "*Damn. It must have gone out when it dropped to the floor. It's a good thing or Elliott might have suffered more serious effects, being so close to the smoke.*" To Wally he said, "Thanks Wally, I owe you one. I'll explain later." After he hung up, Cameron wondered whether Peterson knew the truth about Fishbait's demise.

Cameron returned Nedra's cell phone to her when she came back out, saying, "Well, my friend Wally had some killer news for me."

CHAPTER TEN

It was near noon when Cameron left the office, so he walked home for lunch. Mary was not home and he found a note on the kitchen counter that said, "*I shouldn't have let anybody know I'd be back home today. Got called in to work because two people are out with flu. Don't look for me until at least 8:00. Love Ya. M. (p. s. Let me know how the meeting went.)*"

Cameron made himself a sandwich and sat at the kitchen table to gather his thoughts. He reckoned he should call Raylene right away, but was leery of using the home phone or his cell after his talk with Peterson. He decided to take his chances with Mary's cell phone. She rarely took it to work and he readily found it cradled in its charger. Raylene answered on the second ring.

"Raylene, this is Cameron. There will be some FBI agents coming by to see you today, and I wanted to let you know that you should turn that money you found over to them."

"FBI? What do they want with me?"

"Don't worry; I doubt they're interested in you personally. They know about the money and want to get it from you. They might also ask if you know why your brother had it. Just tell them the truth, like you told me. Speaking of which, you did tell me that you had no contact with Steven and didn't even know he was in jail until they called?"

"Yes, the first I knew was when they called to tell me he was dead."

"You didn't make any trips to the jail before that?"

"Heavens no; like I said, I didn't even know he was there. Besides, I wouldn't of had time to go anyway, with my work schedule."

"And tell me again, why did you have him cremated?"

"I told you he was already cremated before I knew he was dead, don't you remember?"

Cameron could detect the exasperation in Raylene's voice, but needed to feign poor memory to test her story. "That's right, you did. There's been so much going on that I forgot. All right, you take care, and don't worry about the FBI; they're mostly interested in recovering that money."

"Do you think Steven was in something he shouldn't have been?"

"I think he probably was holding the money for somebody else. Like I said, don't worry." Cameron hoped he sounded more convincing to Raylene than he did to himself.

As they said their good-byes, Cameron thought he heard some clicking on the line, and first passed it off as cell-phone interference. Then it then dawned on him that if someone might be tapping his phones, they might also be tapping Raylene's.

CHAPTER ELEVEN

Cameron wanted to sort out the fast-paced confusion of recent events. He needed a refuge where he knew he would be undisturbed, and decided to go to The Retreat.

"The Retreat", as Cameron and Mary called their cabin and wooded acreage on Fulton's River, was not far from Riverport as the crow flies. It was nevertheless a twenty-five minute drive from their home over a circuitous route necessitated by the many swamps, streams and rivers that crisscrossed the county. Cameron counted on the travel time to clear his mind.

The radio blared and Cameron sang along with each classic rock song until he reached the long dirt road that led to the cabin's entry drive. Preferring tranquil silence for the rest of the drive, he cut off the music and began to relax for the first time that day. At the entry drive, he pulled to the narrow shoulder of the road and waited a few minutes. The rooster-tail of dust that had been chasing his truck was catching up and he wanted to give it time to settle. While waiting, he gazed at a field across the road where someone on a tractor was plowing the remains of a depleted summer crop into the ground.

Once the air was reasonably clear, Cameron stepped out to get a better view of the entry drive itself. This side of the road was heavily wooded and it had been a month since his last visit to the cabin. As he feared, a thick tangle of undergrowth now made the drive impassable. His ears burned as he remembered Mary's admonition to him two weeks ago that the road needed maintenance.

Since his truck was partway in the road due to the narrow shoulder, Cameron climbed back in and made a u-turn to the opposite shoulder. He started to step out but realized the truck still sat too far into the roadway. He climbed back in and moved it to a wider section of road-shoulder, and then he got out.

The man on the tractor was closer now, and Cameron recognized him as the farmer who owned the field. Stepping out, he waved to the man and pointed toward the truck, assuming an "OK to leave it here today?" posture as a courtesy. The farmer circled thumb and forefinger into an "OK" sign and kept plowing. Ordinarily, Cameron would have enjoyed socializing with his country neighbor but was glad the man had too much to do today.

On the all-too-frequent occasions when Cameron forgot to maintain the drive, he and Mary took a nearby footpath to the cabin. The path meandered for a few hundred feet but it actually was shorter than the drive. Fortunately, it was still passable and he started hiking in.

He soon came to a part of the path that Mary always dreaded, where it bordered a swamp that harbored countless species of wildlife, including some poisonous snakes and an occasional alligator. Except in times of heavy rain, this part of the path remained high and dry, but the woods were denser on either end and the low canopy sometimes forced them to duck under branches. They only used this route in daylight and even then stepped lightly, Cameron in the lead checking for critters.

After safe passage through the swamp, Cameron climbed the gradual incline that led to the bluff where the cabin stood. Eventually, he emerged from the wooded part of the path onto the grassy back yard of the cabin.

Cameron stopped for a moment and looked at the cabin, already feeling a little more relaxed. The Retreat had been a labor of love for Cameron and Mary. Twenty years earlier, when they bought the property, land prices were more reasonable; Riverport's coastal county was not near the popular vacation and retirement destination it was now.

As relatively cheap as the land was, the monthly payments were hard to come by in the early days of Cameron's practice. To save money, he and Mary began building the cabin by hand with some help from friends and neighbors. Even when they became more financially secure, they continued to work on it themselves, mostly for the exercise, the time together, and the sense of accomplishment. It was built solid enough to withstand the spate of hurricanes that had ravaged the county in the last couple of years.

Cameron let himself in through the side door, and surveyed the realm. The survey did not take long, since the cabin consisted of only three rooms. He was standing in the combination room that spanned the front of the cabin, facing the water. The stone fireplace to his left was flanked by heavy, well stuffed chairs and pine side-tables. Even in summer, when the fireplace was not in use, the scent of wood smoke lingered in the air.

On the right, stainless steel appliances stood out against the rough-hewn cabinetry in the kitchen.

The front wall, the one with the view, consisted mostly of tall mullioned windows, interrupted in the center by a door that led to a deep front porch extending the width of the cabin

Cameron turned and walked down the short hall that separated the bathroom and bedroom at the back. The main power swtichbox was at the end of the hall. Electricity was the only public utility available to the cabin. It had its own well and septic system.

After switching on the power main, Cameron opened a few windows and turned on the ceiling fans to air the place out, then settled into a rocking chair on the front porch. A couple of shots of Jack Daniels could not have had a better effect. He felt the tension drain from every part of his body as he slowly rocked, resting his head on the high back of the chair and breathing deeply. The scents of woods, field and river dispelled the jumbled thoughts that had been troubling him all day. Those problems could wait, if only for a while.

An involuntary spasm jolted Cameron from his reverie. He had drifted into a relaxed near-sleep, the kind that makes the subconscious mind think the body is in free-fall. Deciding his conscious mind was probably clear enough to start working on the puzzle that the day had presented, he stood, rubbed his eyes, and looked out over the front yard.

The view from the porch was one of the best in the county. The front yard sloped down to the Atlantic Intracoastal Waterway. Across the waterway was a narrow barrier island, then the ocean. On clear days, the view extended several miles over the ocean and ships could often be seen making their way to the inlet at Riverport.

Fulton's River, which emptied into the Waterway, was the property's boundary to Cameron's right. Cameron eyed the small dock he had built on the river's edge, making sure his canoe was still safely chained in place. It was an eighteen-foot composite plastic model, dark green, and had held up well over many years of hard use.

One Christmas, Mary had given Cameron a small electric trolling motor for long trips, but paddles were usually sufficient for short fishing excursions.

Now that he felt relaxed enough for quiet contemplation, Cameron was ready to sort out the mass of information that had been hurtling at him. He had been too troubled by it all simply to let it go, as Peterson had suggested. He sat back into the rocker and put his feet up on the rail.

Cameron had developed a method for organizing the masses of information that made up a case file. He would start by developing basic questions, seeing what information was on hand to answer those questions, then determining what information he still needed. Several basic questions emerged on this case.

First, why should he even worry about the case any longer? Several answers came to mind: Raylene had "retained" him to pursue the case, and to his knowledge, he had not yet been relieved of that duty. Next, Peterson's story had altogether too many holes in it; holes that led to more basic questions that he would tackle shortly. And third, if something was interesting enough to sustain his curiosity this long, he couldn't let go of it that easily anyway.

Then there was Fishbait's strange behavior. Why was he wandering that far out in the county so late? He was almost always able to hitch rides with friends or coworkers. Peterson's story about drug running seemed plausible, unless you knew that Fishbait never had a driver's license. He relied on others to get him places, and would barely know how to get a car in gear, much less drive it across the country. No, Fishbait had not been hired to drive drugs from one place to the other.

So, what was Fishbait doing, and why did he have so much cash? It was doubtful he had stolen it. He never struck Cameron as having the nerve to steal it from somebody who had it illegally in the first place, and there had been no recent reports of robberies involving that much cash. Either he was holding it for someone else or he had been paid handsomely for... what? Peterson may have been partly right; Fishbait might have been delivering something to somebody. This question needed more information before an answer could be formed.

The jailhouse provided the next pieces of the puzzle. Who wanted the prisoner dead, and how did they get to him so quickly? How would they have ready access to cyanide-laced cigarettes? Who was the mystery woman who claimed to be Raylene Raeford, and why was Fishbait so quickly cremated, with no investigation into his death?

If the money was merely being held, the owner would most likely wait to reclaim it, or break into Raylene's home to recover it, rather than kill the holder and chance losing it. Cameron reasoned that the money must have been paid for a service. It had to be vital service to warrant a payment that large. Evidently, whoever paid for it felt that Fishbait was too much of a threat to them alive and in police custody.

Some of Peterson's statements could be true. There did appear to be a plant within the sheriff's office, someone who could monitor the prisoners' movements and would know that Fishbait could not make bail. Could it be Elliott Grainger, the jailer? He was in the television room when Fishbait smoked the cigarette. Was he there to be sure it worked? No. If Elliott was an operative, he would have been told to dispose of all the evidence, including the killer cigarette, and he would have looked for it. Besides, Cameron felt that he knew Elliott too well to think he would be part of a criminal conspiracy. Whoever it was must have counted on having plenty of time to make a casual search for the evidence, and would have disposed of it if Cameron had not intervened.

As another question started forming in his mind, Cameron felt a buzzing at his hip. It was Mary's cell phone; he had left his at home. He did not recognize the number calling, but flipped the phone open.

"Hello?"

"Cameron, it's Wally."

"Wally, how did you know to call this number?"

"I couldn't get you on your cell phone or at home, so I called Mary's cell number to find out where you were, and here you are."

"She doesn't like to carry hers for some reason, and I wound up with it today. What's the matter? Your voice sounds shaky."

"Well, I feel shaky. I came in to the lab to catch up on some work today, and when I got there, it was wrecked."

"What do you mean wrecked?"

"Ransacked. Somebody came in and tore it up like they were looking for something."

"Wally, what phone are you using now?"

"I'm at an assistant manager's desk because I didn't want to stay around the lab. I've reported it to the manager, and he's calling the sheriff's office. I'm worried that it might have something to do with what you brought me yesterday."

Cameron hoped the conversation was secure, since neither of them was using his usual phone, but still was circumspect. "Could they have found what I brought you?"

"Not in the lab. I've put it and the test results in my locker, ready to bring to you this afternoon. Evidently they didn't think to look in there, or didn't have time."

"Good. Wally, I'm sorry I got you into this mess." Thinking about the possibility of a plant in the sheriff's department, Cameron continued, "If the deputies question you, I don't want you to lie to them, but try to put them off for a while if you can. I'm not sure who I can trust right now. What I brought you seems to be tied to something that gets messier by the minute."

"Tell you what, there have been some truant school kids vandalizing other businesses out here lately, and in fact that's all it might have been. I'll give them that scent to follow for now, and then play it by ear. I figure I'm already in this about as deep as you are."

"Not quite, but be careful. By all means, don't take that stuff to your house, and see if you can find a more neutral place to put it."

"All right. Take care."

As he flipped the phone shut, it dawned on Cameron that Raylene may be in more danger than he first thought if Fishbait's killers were getting this desperate. Since he did not know when Peterson planned to question her, he could not be sure if the money was safely in the FBI's custody. He dialed her number. An unfamiliar male voice answered.

Cameron replied to the man's abrupt "Who is this?" by stating, "I'm trying to reach Raylene Raeford, do I have the right number?" The man did not reply, but Cameron could hear shuffling sounds, as if the phone was being passed to someone, then a more familiar voice came on the line.

"This is the police, who is trying to reach Ms. Raeford?" Cameron recognized Peterson's voice, but wondered why he did not use his FBI designation.

"Agent Peterson, this is Cameron Scott. I'm glad you're there. Has Raylene handed over some cash to you? I've been getting worried about her safety."

"Mr. Scott, you're a little too late. You have another dead client."

Cameron was stunned, and it took him a while to respond. "What do you mean dead? I just talked to her this morning and advised her to turn the cash over to you."

"I suppose you're talking about the down payment I mentioned to you. We didn't find any of it in the house."

"She said her brother had hidden a wad of cash in his sock drawer, and she had found it. After you told me you were going to see her, I remembered that and called to tell her it would be OK to turn it over to you. She was supposed to have moved it to a safer place in the house."

"We'll look for it some more. But you didn't mention that you knew about the money when we were talking."

"I told you I didn't even think about it until you were gone. You were hitting me with quite a lot of information."

"I'll accept that answer for now," Peterson replied, an obvious tone of doubt in his voice, "but I'll probably have some more questions for you when we get done here."

"That's fine. Can you tell me how she was killed?"

"I didn't say she was killed."

"All right, how did she die?"

"She was killed."

Cameron did not want to play games over how his client lost her life, but evidently, Peterson did for some reason. Cameron asked, "OK, can you tell what killed her?"

"Blunt-force trauma— somebody caved her skull in. We haven't found the weapon yet, and it doesn't look like anybody forced their way in. I'd say it's getting dangerous to retain you as a lawyer, Mr. Scott."

"Seems to me it's been dangerous for my clients to be near law enforcement."

"OK, that's one for me and one for you. We'll call it a draw. I don't believe you have a dog left in this fight, though, so I doubt I'll be seeing any more of you unless I have more questions. Stay close."

"Wasn't planning any trips anyway."

Before hanging up, Peterson took one more swipe: "Heard about your friend's lab. That wouldn't have anything to do with your discussion about 'trains' would it?"

"Something happened at Wally's lab?"

"Uh-huh, and I'm sure you were completely unaware that it was ransacked today."

45

"I guess I did hear something in passing. Been a lot of vandalism out that way lately. Goodbye Agent Peterson."

"Goodbye Mr. Scott." Peterson hung up, leaving Cameron more perplexed than ever.

CHAPTER TWELVE

During his conversation with Peterson, Cameron had wandered inside the cabin away from the noise of passing boats. As he slid the phone back into his pocket, he absentmindedly reached out and turned on the radio that sat on the kitchen counter. It was tuned to a classic rock station that played music he had listened to in high school, and that was as soothing to him as big band music had been to his parents. He had heard the songs so much that he could let them become white noise to aid his concentration.

As the last strains of Jimi Hendrix' "Purple Haze" died away, the DJ cut in with a weather report, and Cameron listened. Tropical Storm Mary's sustained winds were now at fifty miles per hour, and the center was tightening. The storm was located several hundred miles to the southeast of Florida, and no one was venturing a guess as to its probable track yet. A commercial for aluminum siding immediately followed, prompting Cameron to picture countless strips of metal thundering through the air. *They might want to review the positioning of their commercials*," he thought.

The station then aired some local news, and Cameron decided to wait for it to end before resuming his analysis of recent events. There was no mention of Raylene's death, but Cameron figured it was too soon for the media to have been clued into that story anyway. There was mention of a disabled freighter that had been anchored for a few days offshore of Riverport. According to the newscaster, the Coast Guard had boarded and searched the ship, found nothing but ordinary freight, and confirmed that a mechanical system was not functioning. Ship and crew were expected to resume their journey after repair parts arrived. When the music began again, Cameron returned to his thinking session.

It did not take long for Cameron to realize that he was back to his first thought: Why should he even continue with the case? He now had less reason to stay involved, considering he no longer had a client. But he knew he could not let go of it; not yet. Too many questions hung in the air. What happened to Raylene? Surely her death had some tie-in to the money and to Fishbait's demise. And what about Wally? Cameron felt that he might have placed Wally's life in danger by asking him to analyze the cigarette.

Cameron felt sure that someone figured out why he stopped to see Wally, someone who seemed as deadly intent on finding their lost piece of evidence as they had been deadly intent on recovering their cash from Raylene. Apparently the killer or killers found what they came for at Raylene's house, since Peterson was unable to find the money.

While Cameron pondered the immediate questions, a nagging thought lurked in the back of his mind and soon crowded out other concerns. Peterson seemed to know too little, and yet too much. Wally said that his supervisor was just calling the sheriff's office, yet Peterson already knew what had happened. He claimed that Fishbait was supposed to pick up a car the night he was caught, but did not know the man could not drive. And if his agents had not talked to Grainger or gone into the jail, how did they know about Cameron's foray into the TV room?

After taking a deep breath to clear his mind, Cameron looked at his watch. It was nearing five o'clock, and he needed to get home. He and Mary were supposed to meet friends for dinner at six-thirty, and he needed to freshen up before they went. He locked the front door, turned off the radio and then the power, and locked the back door on his way out. Retracing his route on the footpath, he returned to his truck.

Something around his parking spot was not quite right. At first, he could not quite put his finger on it, because nothing appeared out of place on the surface. But then he noticed something so subtle that it was barely detectable. After making his u-turn earlier he had to pull off twice to park the truck. The first time, he saw that he was not safely off the traveled road. Since there was an eroded spot on the roadside immediately in front of the truck, he pulled back onto the roadway to go around it, and then pulled all the way onto the shoulder. His first set of tire tracks were gone, along with the tracks leading up to his current spot. Thinking at first that some wind had blown sand over the tracks, he took a closer look and saw that someone had obliterated them deliberately, apparently using a tree branch or other means to sweep the marks off.

No other tire marks were visible on either road shoulder. Cameron could only surmise that someone had pulled off the road behind his truck for some reason, then erased their tracks upon leaving, not realizing they had already erased another set of tracks with their own tires. One the main roadway, no particular set of tire tracks was distinguishable from the others.

Cameron hurried to look in the truck bed to see if anything was out of place. Some road dirt and a few bits of bark from the last firewood load it had carried were all that showed in the bed. There was no sign of entry at the cab either. The doors were still locked, everything was in its usual place, and there appeared to be no damage. Although the hood latch was inside the locked cab, he nevertheless pulled it and raised the hood to see if anyone had tampered with the engine. Nothing amiss. Finally, he inspected the gas cap for any sign that something may have been poured into the tank. Still no sign of tampering. Cameron decided that he might just be getting paranoid after all the recent happenings, so he punched the remote start button on his keyring and climbed in for the ride home.

Had Cameron looked into a dark recess under the truck bed, near the rear bumper, he might have found the small transponder attached there.

CHAPTER THIRTEEN

It was ten after six by the time Cameron got home, barely enough time to change clothes before leaving for dinner. After an initial scolding from Mary, he promised to explain his tardiness as they drove her car to their friends' house.

On the way, Cameron related an abridged version of the day's events to Mary, including his trip to the cabin, and the absence of the second set of tire tracks. They both concluded that he may have tried to read too much into the incident on the roadside, since no one seemed to have tampered with the truck. Mary expressed concern for his safety, but he did his best to assure her that he probably would have little more to do with the case, short of answering a few of Peterson's questions.

The dinner date was with old friends Larry and Sandy Gullege. Sandy, a petite blond with an easy smile, met them at the door and escorted them to the den, where Larry was pouring drinks. He took pride in knowing everyone's favorite and handed a white Zinfandel to Mary and a seven-and-seven to Cameron as soon as they walked in.

Larry generally despised lawyers, having lost the protracted litigation that followed the breakup of his first marriage. When he first met Cameron, Larry mistook the lawyer's reserved demeanor for snobbishness and was prepared to despise him as well. For his part, Cameron thought the large man's overbearing, boisterous manner was an affectation. However, long-time friends Sandy and Mary strongly urged their husbands to socialize, breaking the ice by getting them to talk about their mutual interests. Cameron thawed when he learned that Larry was a skilled guitar player who could help him improve his own guitar technique. And Larry warmed to Cameron's past career as a park ranger that meshed well with his own love of the outdoors.

Despite the friendship that grew between them, Larry could never resist assailing Cameron with every lawyer joke he heard, his ruddy face reddening deeper as he howled at his own humor. If the joke was fresh and funny, Cameron laughed just as hard as Larry. But if it was a clinker that he already heard too may times, he would counter with a deadpan look that made Larry laugh even harder.

Before anyone could sit down, Larry launched into a lawyer joke he heard earlier in the day. It was both new and funny, and he was rewarded with a burst of laughter all around. As they sipped their drinks, Mary asked Larry about the ships he had brought in that day.

As one of a few skilled river pilots in the area, Larry had spent close to twenty years guiding ships of all sizes past treacherous ocean shoals, through the inlet at Riverport, and up river to the port of Whittington or the military munitions terminal just past Riverport. Larry took his job seriously, yet almost always found some humor in the things that went on around him as he piloted the ships. His rendition of the day's events kept everyone amused while they finished their drinks and then Cameron drove them to the restaurant in Mary's car.

Dinner was a relaxing diversion and the evening passed quickly. After dinner, Cameron and Mary dropped Larry and Sandy off at their house and drove home. After spending an evening in conversation, they were content to listen to the car radio. During a news break, a weather reporter updated the status of Tropical Storm Mary. Cameron shook his head, remembering that he forgot to buy batteries in his hurry to get home from the cabin. Once more, time, thought and opportunity had failed to converge. Maybe tomorrow.

After hearing the weather report, Mary said, "You know, if that storm heads this way, I'll be living at the plant, coordinating emergency operations."

"But of course," Cameron replied offhandedly, "and I'll be living at the office." He was referring to his practice of riding out hurricanes there. None of the storms they had experienced so far exceeded category three in strength. Storms of that magnitude were dangerous, but bearable in the solidly built historic structure that housed Cameron's office. It sat on higher ground than their home site—"higher" in coastal Riverport being just twenty-five feet above sea level—and the building never suffered flooding in its hundred-year history.

Mary sighed and said, "I hate when we have to lose contact during the storms. I know the plant is built to withstand them, but I worry about you."

Cameron said, "If there's the slightest chance the storm will go to category four or five I'm out of here, OK? And I'll call you as soon as possible."

Mary smiled while she lightly stroked his cheek with the back of her hand. After he wrapped one arm around her and pulled her close to him, they maintained comfortable silence the rest of the way home.

As he prepared for bed that night, Cameron wondered what surprises were waiting in the days ahead.

CHAPTER FOURTEEN

Fortunately, Sunday was quiet. Cameron and Mary went to church in the morning and spent the afternoon watching television at home. Time, thought and opportunity finally converged in the evening and Cameron remembered to pick up batteries, although the weather report showed little change in the storm's direction or intensity.

Cameron was in the office at his normal time next morning, and had a stack of messages waiting. At the top was one marked "URGENT" in red. He raised one eyebrow as he looked at Nedra, who was behind her desk waiting to speak.

"He called three times this morning. What's this Peterson guy working on?"

"My nerves right now. I'm surprised he didn't call me at home yesterday."

"He said he would have tried, but he knew you were out late Saturday night."

"Figures. He seems to know quite a bit about my comings and goings."

"Is he family or something?"

"He's a lot like an obnoxious cousin, but no, he's FBI. He's the one you saw here Saturday. Says he's working on a major drug case, but that information doesn't leave this office."

"I understand, but why's he bugging you?"

"Something to do with what Fishbait was doing on the night he broke into the store. And that's about all I'd better tell you for now."

"Gotcha. No more questions from me."

During the conversation with Nedra, Cameron had been leafing through his message slips. Most were routine matters; the secretaries could respond to several and his associate, Ben Gravely could answer the rest. Suddenly his attention was riveted on one of the slips. It was undated, but the caller had been Raylene Raeford. The time of the call was not marked on the slip, so he quickly asked Nedra when it came in.

"I'm not sure," she replied, "it was on my voicemail. I'm sorry I didn't get the time on that message, but the phone started ringing in the middle of me writing it, and I forgot. I can get the time, though, because I didn't erase the voicemail yet; I thought you needed to listen to it."

"All right, go ahead and play it back."

She punched the buttons to recall the message. The machine's automated voice gave the date, which was Saturday, and said the call time was three thirty-two. Raylene's voice could then be heard, saying, "Mr. Scott, I don't have very much time to talk, and this is the only number I have for you. If I get gone, look in the cinder block." The message ended abruptly.

Nedra apologized again for failing to write out the message.

"Don't worry about it," Cameron absolved, "Were there any other messages from Raylene?"

"That was it."

"OK, thanks." He then told her who should get each of the remaining message slips and instructed her to hold his calls for now.

After shutting his office door, Cameron sat down to try to reconstruct Saturday's timeline. He knew he had first talked to Raylene somewhere between noon and one o'clock, but when did he make the second call, the one that Peterson answered? He could not think of a ready reference because he had lost track of time that afternoon until he finally looked at his watch around five. As he tried to find some sort of hint at the time of his call to Raylene, his cell phone began buzzing. It was Mary, asking if he had seen the paper yet about Raylene's death. He had not, and she told him the gist of the story that she'd been reading on coffee break.

"According to the paper" she said, "an anonymous tipster told authorities that Raylene kept large amounts of cash around the house and the police suspect that one of Steven's drug-using friends murdered her while searching for the money. Time of death was estimated to be about one p.m. Saturday. Someone struck her in the back of the head with a heavy object but they haven't found that yet. Riverport Police are conducting further investigations, and want to question the source who knew about the cash. There was other comment about the tragedy of two deaths in the same family only a few days apart."

"Fishbait finally gets a mention," said Cameron. He thought, but did not say, *"and the FBI does not."*

"It wasn't you that tipped 'the authorities' off about the cash was it?" asked Mary.

"Afraid so. Peterson's already been calling me, probably to get more info about that. I'm surprised he wasn't on the office doorstep this morning. Listen, don't worry. I think they just haven't found the money yet, and he wants to know if I have a clue as to where she put it. I've gotta go. Love you."

"Love you, too. Be careful, I'm too old to have to break in a new husband."

"OK, bye bye."

Hitting the off button on the cell phone, he stared at the ID screen while gathering his thoughts. His gaze wandered idly over the screen for a few seconds but suddenly came into sharp focus on one set of numbers. The phone was telling him what time the call from Mary came in.

Excitedly, Cameron rushed out to his truck, where he had plugged in Mary's cell phone to recharge. He grabbed her phone, flipped it open and punched the "recent calls" button, then selected "dialed calls". Within the list of dialed calls was Raylene's number. Scrolling down to her number, he hit the "view" button and there was the answer to his timeline question; he made the second call at three forty-seven. Raylene was alive at three thirty-two when the voicemail message was recorded and dead no more than fifteen minutes later when Peterson answered her phone. She must have known something was imminent and being unable to talk directly to Cameron, left her cryptic message. He wondered why the newspaper reported her time of death being more than two hours earlier.

As Cameron stood by his truck digesting these new revelations, another pickup truck pulled into his parking lot, driven by a man in a short-sleeve plaid shirt.

CHAPTER FIFTEEN

"I see you took my advice," Cameron called to Peterson, who was climbing out of the truck. Cameron quickly flipped the phone shut and closed his truck door.

"Yup, trying to blend in," responded Peterson. "You just getting to work?"

"Nah, had to put something in my truck."

"Wouldn't be about ten grand in cash would it?" Peterson was laughing with his voice, but not his eyes.

"Still haven't found the money Raylene told me about?" Cameron wondered how Peterson knew the amount, since he hadn't mentioned it to him.

"I'm not sure it was ever in the house. We tore the place apart on your word, but there's nothing there."

Motioning for Peterson to precede him into the building, Cameron asked, "What brings you here, then? By the number of messages you left, you seemed awfully anxious to see me. I thought you'd have been to my house yesterday, in fact."

"I had too much to do yesterday, and up until a short time ago this morning, I've been tied up answering to my boss in D.C. He's been chewing my ass for losing the 'Underground Railroad' drug connection here. Anyway, I only have a few more questions for you."

"I guess you're about done down here then?"

"I've still got to wrap up a few loose ends, then start over." By this time they were both seated in Cameron's office.

Peterson continued, "I guess you've seen the official report of Ms. Raeford's death in the paper."

"I got a synopsis, anyway. It still puzzles me why you don't think she had the money in the house. Didn't you—or the local police, according to the paper—say she was killed by someone looking for money?"

"Like I said, that's the official report. We think she was actually done in by the same people who killed her brother. I guess they thought she knew too much. We want them to think we're on the wrong trail, so maybe they'll try to reactivate the supply route."

Cameron said, "So you think her brother didn't die of natural causes..." and then hesitated before asking his next question, "Does anybody know what killed him?"

"We've known that since the night he died. Cyanide poisoning. We're just not sure how they got it in him."

Cameron resisted the schoolboy urge to jump up and say "I know, I know." Instead he said, "I thought he got sent off for cremation before an autopsy could be performed."

"That's another official story, again hoping they'd reactivate the supply route. We actually took custody of the body as soon as we found out he died and had an autopsy done. The cyanide was concentrated in his lungs, so we know it was inhaled, but there was no evidence left at the scene to show how it got there. I'm afraid the plant in the sheriff's office got to it first."

Cameron was beginning to formulate his own idea of who the plant might be. He still did not feel secure enough about Peterson to divulge what he knew about the cigarette.

"The only question I have for you, Mr. Scott, is whether Ms. Raeford said anything to you that could give you any idea of where her brother's money might have gone."

"She didn't say a thing to me other than what I've told you." Cameron was telling the truth the way opposing witnesses often did on the stand; he told the truth but not the whole truth. Sure, Raylene left a message about the cinderblock, but she did not **say** it to him directly. All the same, he had an idea that someone might have been listening in on Raylene's short voicemail connection and that Peterson was not through with him yet. He also had an idea that the police searched more than the interior of Raylene's house and still came up dry.

While the two conversed, Cameron noticed that Peterson was scanning his desktop, apparently looking for any bit of information that might help him. Cameron was glad that he always kept his

57

message slips face-side down so clients could not read them. Sensing that Peterson had no more questions for him, Cameron asked one more of his own: "Why are you telling me so much of the unofficial story?"

"Mr. Scott, I want you to understand how dangerous this whole affair is. I trust that you know that it's in your best interest to drop out of it now and not repeat any of what I've shared with you."

"Warning taken. I don't suppose I have any reason to bother with it any more, really."

"That's a good attitude, Mr. Scott. Good day."

"Take care. Drop by some time when you can stay for dinner."

They both laughed uneasily as Cameron saw Peterson out the door.

Certain that Raylene left her cryptic message for a good reason, Cameron felt he owed her an effort to decipher its meaning.

CHAPTER SIXTEEN

The rest of Cameron's day was routine, consisting of a couple of real estate closings, a will signing, and some legal research. Soon, it was time to leave. Mary was on a twelve-hour shift and would not be home until eight, so he stopped at his favorite local diner for the day's supper special.

He ate rather mechanically, his thoughts being on Raylene's message. Surely she must have thought the simple mention of one cinder block would trigger something in his memory. He strained to recall the brief telephone conversation with her and suddenly paused, a forkful of mashed potato poised in midair, as he recalled her remark about Fishbait trying to repair the barbecue pit. What had she said? Something about him trying to fix the brick and block. That was it; the barbecue pit must have had a brick exterior, but a cinderblock core.

Even if they had intercepted her voicemail message, the police might have no idea that the back yard barbecue would have cinder blocks in it. Cameron decided to wait until nightfall to test his theory, so he finished his meal and went home.

By dark, Mary had come home, and was settled into an easy chair reading a mystery novel. On the pretense of needing to finish some business at the office, Cameron left the house and drove away in his truck. He hated lying to Mary but did not want her worrying over his welfare.

While driving down the street he kept a careful lookout in his rearview mirror, watching for any sign that he was being followed. He could see no movement, nor did he see any unfamiliar vehicles in the neighborhood. As an extra precaution, he took a circuitous route, cutting across some narrow alleys, even doubling back on himself.

Finally he parked a few blocks from Raylene's house, removed a flashlight from the glove compartment and walked the rest of the way, peering around for signs of company. Satisfied that he was alone as he reached her house, he slipped into the back yard.

Enough ambient light shone in the yard for him to see his way to the barbecue pit without the flashlight. Upon reaching the structure, he immediately began feeling around for any loose bricks. In the outside rear, toward the left center, some of the bricks wobbled so he shined the light on that area. Although the masonry on the rest of the structure was sound, the bricks in the lit area were poorly aligned and had bits of mortar missing. A pull on one of the bricks revealed that the mortar was not even attached.

Cameron continued to remove bricks until he could see the outline of a cinder block behind them. The mortar around this block had also deteriorated, and it pulled out rather easily. The block scraped loudly as it slid, so Cameron stopped, listened and peered into the darkness. He heard nothing and saw no movement.

Cameron laid the cinder block on the grass, and then crouched down to shine his light into the hole where it had been. He smiled to himself as he saw the gleam of a plastic bag. He lifted the bag out, opened it, and removed the contents; ten stacks of hundred dollar bills, ten to a stack, and a small piece of folded notepaper. When he opened the paper he detected pencil marks, so he shined the light directly on it. It read, "*I'm L2 and Steven was L1. Trust P*" in hastily scrawled lettering. He scarcely had time to fathom the meaning of the words when he was startled by a voice behind him.

"I'll take custody of that now, Mr. Scott," said the voice, "just stay crouched and turn very slowly with your hands behind your head."

Cameron did as instructed. He had dropped the light on the ground, but as he turned he could tell even in the faint ambient light that a pistol was pointed at his forehead. He could also tell that the pistol was in the hand of Agent Gene Peterson.

CHAPTER SEVENTEEN

Peterson directed Cameron to move away from the barbecue pit and the cash. Cameron, still crouching, crabwalked several steps away as Peterson kept the pistol trained on him.

Peterson picked up the flashlight, money, and notepaper, glancing briefly at the message before turning his gaze back to Cameron. He said, "I just don't know what to do with you, Mr. Scott. I can't seem to convince you to get yourself out of this case, so I guess I'll have to do something else." He stuffed the money and note into his pockets.

Cameron asked, "And what will be the grounds for an arrest?"

"Oh, I could think of plenty, but who said anything about an arrest? Stand up, Mr. Scott, and start walking toward the house. And keep your hands behind your head."

Events felt surreal to Cameron as he thought, "*Is he planning to kill me? I can't believe this; he's going to waste me right here at Raylene's and make it look like I was part of the drug operation.*"

As they reached the back door of the house, Peterson said, "All right, now turn left and walk toward the next yard. My vehicle's on the next street over."

Cameron briefly thought of running, but knew that could earn him a bullet in the back. While they walked past the next house he ventured to question, "How'd you know to find me here? I checked to make sure I wasn't followed. Have you been waiting here all the time, hoping I'd show up?"

"No, and shut up and keep walking. We're almost to the car." As the vehicle came into view, Cameron saw that Peterson was using his government-issue sedan again.

When they reached the car, Cameron stopped by the back bumper, assuming that he was about to be put in the trunk, taken to a remote location, and shot. Peterson almost ran into him but quickly backed away, saying, "What the hell are you doing?"

"I just thought I'd make it easy for you. Aren't you going to stuff me in the trunk?"

Peterson pushed Cameron to the front passenger door and barked, "You idiot, you've been watching too much television. Just get in the car." He slipped his pistol back into its shoulder holster as he opened the door. Bewildered, Cameron dropped into the seat. Then Peterson scurried to the driver's side, taking his place behind the wheel.

An open notebook computer sprang to life as Peterson started the car, its screen turned toward him. As he got underway, Peterson turned the screen so that Cameron could see a grid of named streets on it, which he recognized as the neighborhood they were driving through. On Raylene's street, a couple of blocks away from her house, a red dot blinked on and off.

"I didn't have to sit out here waiting for you," said Peterson, "You led me here. When you took your country drive Saturday, one of my men planted a transponder under your truck after you hiked into the woods. I've known where you were ever since, except when you drove your wife's car last night."

"So your man erased my tracks. I knew I wasn't losing my mind."

"Erased your tracks?"

"Yeah, I pulled off the road twice on that side. If your guy parked over my first set of tracks, he probably obliterated those and thought he only erased his own tracks before he left. At first I got suspicious when I noticed the missing tire prints, then I figured I was just getting paranoid."

"You're more observant than I thought, Mr. Scott."

"And less paranoid than I thought. So what are your plans for me now? Will anybody ever be able to find me?"

"You might have noticed that you aren't cuffed and my weapon is holstered, so relax; we don't have far to go."

Both men fell silent as Peterson drove into the countryside. Cameron tried to sort out Raylene's phone message. Maybe it wasn't really her who called his office. Peterson or his men could have killed her earlier and had someone leave the message; maybe the same phony Raylene that left tainted cigarettes for Fishbait. But

Nedra and Cameron both knew Raylene's voice, having frequented the restaurant where she worked. They would not have been easily fooled by an impersonator. Then again, they were concentrating on the message and time of the call rather than the voice of the caller. Without realizing it, Cameron let out a heavy sigh.

As if reading Cameron's mind, Peterson looked at him and said, "You only think you're confused now. Just wait a few minutes."

After a while they were out of town, traveling down a back road unfamiliar to Cameron. Shortly, Peterson slowed the car, cut off the lights and turned onto a dirt drive flanked by thick woods. The drive was so overgrown that Cameron had not even noticed it. He heard weeds and brush slap the car's undercarriage as Peterson slowly drove forward about a hundred yards, seeing his way by moonlight, then stopped in front of a dark derelict farmhouse. As he got out of the car, Peterson pressed something in his shirt pocket, mumbled a few words, and cocked his head as if listening. Next he hurried around and opened Cameron's door, saying, "We're going in the house, you first."

Having no idea who might be watching, or waiting in the woods for him if he ran, Cameron simply walked to the back door of the house as directed, opened it, and stepped in. Following close behind, Peterson closed the door, stood listening again for a few seconds, and then snapped on a small penlight. He guided Cameron through the house to a back room that appeared to be a kitchen. In the dim light Cameron could make out the form of someone sitting at a table waiting for them. Peterson shined the light on a chair and motioned for Cameron to sit down, then sat next to him.

As Peterson turned the light toward the face of the man at he table, he said dryly, "I believe you two have met." Cameron stared dumbfounded; the other man was Deputy Elliott Grainger.

CHAPTER EIGHTEEN

Grainger was in the middle of removing a small hearing device from his ear. The earpiece was connected to a small walkie-talkie in his hand. Cameron realized that Peterson must have been wearing a wireless earpiece and collar-microphone, and got an "all-clear" from Grainger before and after entering the house.

Having assured himself that all the shades in the room were drawn, Peterson switched on a small lamp in the center of the table and said, "All right Mr. Scott, let's see if we can uncomplicate the past few days for you before we complicate your life even further. I'm sure you've deduced that I haven't been altogether forthcoming with you. No, no need to answer. Deputy Grainger and I have been playing a little game of charades with you and just about everybody else in this county because, quite frankly, we don't know who we can trust. I'm not even sure I can trust some of my own agents at this point"

"You don't trust any of your fellow lawmen, either of you?"

"I didn't exactly say that; I said we're not **sure** if we can trust some of them. I knew I could trust Deputy Grainger and Raylene Raeford; Grainger for several reasons and Raylene because I knew her parents to the day they died, and have known her and her brother since they were small children. Their father, Major Raeford, was my commanding officer when I was a chopper pilot in 'Nam, and we kept up with each other when we got back home. He saw something in me that I couldn't at the time, and insisted I go to law school and apply to the F.B.I. once I had my degree. Before that, I'd been drifting from job to job for a couple years."

"I remember the Bureau recruiting at my school when I was in second-year law."

"The Bureau's been good to me, but I'm ready for an early retirement. I've got to see this project through before I can even think about retiring, though. Anyway, the Major and his wife were killed by a drunk driver a few years after my graduation. Raylene was eighteen by then, and Steven was fourteen and pure trouble. Who knows why some kids just seem to go the wrong route? Raylene tried to be his surrogate mother and wound up devoting her life to him. What little inheritance they had went fast, so she had to work to keep them up and couldn't get to college. It's a shame, because she would have done well. Steven started following the commercial fishing trade when he would work and eventually they wound up here."

Cameron interjected, "I know you said you'd clear things up, but I'm probably more confused. Did you or your people not dispose of Fishbait and Raylene?"

"I had no direct connection with either death. In fact, I didn't even know they were in danger until I learned that Steven got arrested. Even that might not have drawn me to Riverport if it weren't for the peculiar circumstances. I recognized the pattern behind Steven's death and got here as fast as I could. I've thoroughly checked out Deputy Grainger and he's been helping me, but they got to Steven before either of us could do anything about it. By the way, despite his good-ol'-boy act, Elliott here is college material, and I've been getting on his case about working on a degree."

Grainger blushed but said nothing. Cameron gave him a sideways glance, knowing that he had been on Elliott's case already for the same reason. Cameron then asked them both, "What do you mean 'they' got to Steven?" Grainger just nodded back toward Peterson.

Peterson responded, "I'll get to that in just a minute. But first I want you to understand that there's no way I would have put either of their lives in danger if I could have helped it. I think you found out from your friend Wally how Steven was killed."

"So it was you who tore up his lab?"

"Let's just say I have a few more operatives here I can trust, and one of them eventually found where Wally hid the cigarette. But don't worry, your friend isn't in trouble. At any rate Raylene really did bring the original pack of cigarettes to the jail, so Elliott assumed they were safe. The problem is, the story I told you about someone in the sheriff's office being a plant is true. Someone switched packs after she brought them."

"I think I might have figured out who the plant is."

"I think Elliott and I have as well, but the man has disappeared. He's either gone to another assignment or suffered the same fate as Steven and Raylene."

"Would the man be the second jailer on duty that night, Wagoner?"

"That would be him. You can tell me later how you came to that conclusion; there's still too much to tell you right now. But there is time for you to call someone who's probably worried." Peterson sat back in his chair to allow his words to sink in.

With a start, Cameron said, "Oh my gosh, Mary's probably wondering what the hell's keeping me at the office this long."

As Cameron took out his cell phone, Peterson said, "Exactly. Just tell her I came by to ask a few more questions, and you'll be home a little later than you thought."

"You mean I'll be going home?"

"Yes, Mr. Scott, you're going home. Now go ahead and call."

Cameron called Mary, gave his apologies for being so late, repeated the excuse Peterson had given him, then told her not to wait up and he would try not to be too late.

When the call was finished, Peterson continued, "You don't know how much it pained me to see what happened to Steven and Raylene. I assigned my one female agent, Tanya, to watch over Raylene. Tanya's fairly new so I didn't think they'd gotten to her yet. I was wrong and that's why I no longer know who I can trust, except my select operatives."

"There's 'they' again. You're going to have to tell me who the mystery people are. In the meantime why can't this new agent tell you who bashed in Raylene's head?"

"It was Tanya herself who did it."

"For Pete's sake, man, why don't you arrest her?"

"I can't. At least not now. My whole operation would be in jeopardy if I did that. For now I have to act like I believe her story that someone snuck past her."

"You do understand that you're making no sense here."

Grainger finally spoke. "Mr. Peterson, I think you better tell him who 'they' are."

CHAPTER NINETEEN

After considering Grainger's request, Peterson nodded in agreement and continued, "Mr. Scott, I've known and trusted Raylene Raeford a long time. I only wish she hadn't got herself mixed up in this thing. I imagine she had no idea who she really was working for but she probably thought the money would give her and Steven a boost. For some reason she trusted you. She left that note hinting at what she and Steven did for the organization and telling you to trust me. If she trusted you, I suppose I should too."

"Wait a minute, you're trying to tell me that you're the 'P' she referred to in the note?"

"Who else do you think it would be? She tried to give enough information to get you interested without giving too much away to anyone who might casually find the money and note. I was the only one listening to the wire on her phone, and she knew I was listening."

"How did she know that?"

"I told her"

"You did?"

"Yup. It's important for you to know that the note you found with the money was meant for both of us. I think she wanted us to work together, and that's why she left that voicemail for you."

"So you knew about that, too?"

"Of course. I got to her house as fast as I could after hearing it, but it was already too late."

"OK, so what is it you want to trust me with Agent Peterson?"

"Gene."

"What?"

"Call me Gene. And I hope you don't mind if I call you by your first name."

"You can call me anything you want at this point, just get on with it… Gene!"

"I'm trying but I've had to keep this information so close that it's hard for me to relate it to a stranger; even Elliott hasn't heard all of this. You see, a shadow government has arisen within our government."

"Oh, well, that makes it all clear. I never thought anybody was really in charge anyway."

"I know you're joking, Cameron, but you've just about summed up their philosophy."

"They who, and what philosophy?"

"A small group of renegade career bureaucrats. They believe we no longer have a constitutional government no matter what party is in power."

Cameron settled back in his chair and stared blankly, the meaning of Peterson's words still eluding him.

"You're having the same reaction I had when I first heard this, Cameron, so don't feel too stupid," Peterson laughed. It was the first genuine laugh Cameron had heard from him.

Peterson went on, "I'm sure you learned in Constitutional law class about our country's second, bloodless, revolution in 1787."

"The Constitutional Convention, yes."

"It was called to save a confederation of states that was falling apart at the seams because there was no real central government to stitch them together."

Cameron responded, "The delegates wanted the security of common defense, stable commerce, and whatnot, but most were extremely wary of a far-off, powerful government. They'd just gotten rid of one of those in the form of the King."

"You did pay attention in class, Cameron. You probably recall that they were only supposed to meet and discuss ways of unifying the states, but instead invented a whole new government. Once they'd hammered out a constitution, they felt confident that it had enough checks and balances to prevent abuses of power."

Cameron warmed to the concept, adding, "But the states refused to ratify the new Constitution without further checks on government power. They insisted on adding amendments to restrain the central government more."

"A-plus, Cameron. Now some time ago our renegade career folks held their own secret 'constitutional convention' of sorts. They feared that we were rapidly producing our own permanent 'ruling class' of politicians. Apparently there was a lot of discussion about politicians in all three branches of government ignoring the checks and balances, and bending the laws to ensure each others' longevity."

"And they didn't see their own bureaucracy as part of the problem?"

"On the contrary. The core group considered most politicians of either party to be self-interested idiots. They saw themselves as the only ones with enough governmental insight, intelligence, and expertise to put things back on track."

"I noticed you said 'core group'," interrupted Cameron. "How many are in this organization, and what, by the way, do they call themselves?"

"To my knowledge, they purposely adopted no name, probably to avoid identification and to avoid looking like one more fringe political party. I don't know how many are in the central core by now; that's the most closely guarded secret of the group. It started with a few eggheads who were solely interested in the intellectual exercise, thinking they could change things from within. A few people who drifted in and out of the group knew the original members. That's how we know they even exist. At that point, no one paid much attention to them. Eventually others entered the fold who were less benign, and much more secretive."

Cameron stopped him. "And what do you think about all this, being a career government employee?"

"I think I'm like Deputy Grainger and most other career grunts. We're too busy worrying about our jobs and our own lives to worry which politician is screwing us at a given time. I guess I might feel the same way sometimes about the politicians; one party likes to tax and spend and the other likes to borrow and spend, and they're both pretty self-interested in their own ways. But I guess the current system beats what anybody else has come up with."

"So you figure 'if it ain't broke, don't fix it'?"

"I'm sure there's a lot of fixing that could be done. I just don't like the tools these folks are trying to use."

"You don't know who's in this new group that took over? Are the original members afraid to talk?"

"I suppose if they were alive, they'd be glad to tell us what they knew. Unfortunately, they're all gone."

"Gone? As in dead?"

"As in dead. I told you, this new core group is less benign. I suppose a better way to put it is to say they are ruthless, and callous up to a point. Although each death was made to look natural or by ordinary misfortune, I guarantee that each one of the founders was murdered by the newcomers. Then they hunted and destroyed those who'd drifted in and out, but not before I discovered that the organization existed and who the founders were. So far though, they've been ruthless within the organization but they've done no harm to the general public that I can determine."

"Where do you fit in?"

"President Mills has given me complete authority and discretion to assemble the team to unravel and stop this organization. As far as the Bureau knows, I'm working on a secret Homeland Security assignment."

"With all this going on, how does the President know he can trust a career government employee like you with that task?"

"Ordinarily he wouldn't. But we're related, albeit distantly. Only a few close family members even know that. Even so, that in itself wouldn't be enough but for the fact that he might not even be here if it weren't for me."

"What do you mean?"

"On one of the rare occasions when our families visited each other, we were both kids, about eight years old. On one visit, while our parents talked we went upstairs to his room so he could show me his comic book collection. Like about every other kid, we were fascinated with super-heroes, and we got to talking about how great it would be to have those kinds of powers. He suddenly got it into his head that if he just had a cape on, he could leap out the window and fly away, like his favorite hero."

Cameron and Grainger looked at each other, each with a vision of the President flying out the window, and began to snicker.

Peterson, on the verge of laughter himself, held up his hand to silence them. "I know, I know, but you have to remember we were only eight. Kids can be pretty dumb at that age and they really want to believe they can do it. Anyway, he tied a towel around his neck for a cape and before I knew it, he was diving out the open window. I guess he'd have dived straight to the ground with broken arms or worse to show for it, if the towel hadn't caught on a nail. Instead, he tumbled out the window and wound up hanging by his neck. In the short time it took me to get to the window and look down, his face was already turning purple."

Cameron interrupted, "So you pulled him back up?"

"Hell no, I didn't have the strength at that age."

"Well we know he lived through it, so what did you do?"

"I didn't do a thing right then. The towel ripped where the nail caught it and let go. He flew all right, but it was straight down, feet first. By then he had passed out and he fell kind of like a rag doll into the soft flower bed, which might have kept him from breaking a leg."

"So how did you get to be the hero of the story?"

"After he landed he wasn't moving or breathing. I climbed out the window so fast I didn't have time to think about the height. Then I hung by my hands from the sill for a second before doing a drop and roll, just missing him. We'd been learning about artificial respiration in Cub Scouts so I rolled him over and started pushing on his back and raising his arms, like you did drowning victims in those days."

"You didn't holler for help?"

"Like I said, we were kids. I was afraid we'd get into too much trouble. It didn't even occur to me how much trouble there would be if he didn't make it. Anyway, to cut it short, he did start breathing again. Once he regained his color and found out nothing was broken, we swore we would keep each other out of trouble and not tell our parents. Since they were all in the kitchen at the back of the house they didn't hear the commotion, and thought we'd just gone out by the front door when they found us outside."

Peterson leaned back and put his feet up on the chair next to him before continuing, "Funny, I guess in a way he got his superpowers. At least to a majority of the voters he's a superhero of sorts now. It's a shame the harmless group of renegade bureaucrats got shoved out, because he probably would have agreed with them. He's always been somewhat of a Washington outsider. Well now Cameron, after that, what other blanks can I fill in for you?"

Cameron took a few moments to collect his thoughts. There was a lot to absorb in so short a time. Finally, he said, "Who actually put the tracking device on my truck, and how did you know to trust him?"

Grainger answered, "I'm sorry, Mr. Scott, but that was me. Mr. Peterson figured even if you did see me you wouldn't get too suspicious, since you know me. That was the first chance I had to get to your truck without anybody seeing me."

"OK, what did Raylene and Steven have to do with this, and what're L1 and L2? That's what we called first and second year law students, but I know she wasn't referring to law school."

Peterson answered this time. "This group has four categories of operation as far as I can tell. They assign a number to each category, or 'Level' as they call it. Steven was Level One and Raylene was Level Two; that's where the 'L1' and 'L2' come from. Level Two consists of recruiters, who never have direct contact with people in the third or fourth category. I got that much out of Raylene before she... well, while she was still alive. Level Ones are runners or messengers. Sometimes they drive, sometimes they walk. They may go by boat or plane at times. It's an elaborate chain that takes several links to pass a message among upper levels, who seem almost paranoid about usual means of communication. Raylene recruited Steven to deliver a message, and it must have been an important one considering the payment they were getting. The ten thousand you found was the first half."

"But how did Raylene and Steven let themselves get mixed up with anybody that dangerous?"

"From what I've discovered so far, most people in the lower categories have no idea who they're working for. It looks like they're picked because they have financial trouble. I'm not sure yet how the group knows they need money, but I suspect they've hacked into credit bureau records and who knows what else on the internet. That would be the Level Threes at work."

"And their job is...?"

"They plan and enforce. The details are a lot sketchier past Level Two, but I'm pretty certain they get their orders from the Level Fours then plan the details and get them carried out. I haven't been able to link the upper levels directly to a given event yet."

"You said they plan and enforce; what do you mean by 'enforce'?"

"Steven and Raylene are examples. If anybody in Level One or Two screws up, they're eliminated. I doubt that any of the lowest levels have any idea that's what they signed on for; they're mostly in it for the money. Usually the person who screwed up is the only one to suffer but Raylene went against protocol and recruited her own

72

brother. That was a fatal mistake for her since she obviously paid for his error as well."

"But doesn't that give you a link to a Level Three person, knowing your fellow F.B.I. agent was an enforcer in Raylene's case?"

"Unfortunately, no. Level Threes usually don't enforce directly; they make sure it gets done by a different set of Level Two personnel, who work on a contract basis. Now I know that Tanya, the agent I left with Raylene, is one of those enforcers. By the way, she's been put on administrative leave, supposedly for letting someone get past her to Raylene. She'll be watched until it's safe to have her arrested."

"If nobody knows who anybody else is, how does anything get done?"

"Their communication system is so complex I haven't completely figured it out. Even the Level Fours don't seem to all know each other; they operate in small groups with a sophisticated system to recognize each others' messages. It's funny, but here in the computer age they rarely use the internet to communicate because they don't want anyone to track them electronically. Once when Raylene and I were alone, she told some of what she knew about the communication system but I think the note you found behind the cinderblock had a another clue for me."

Peterson fished the folded note that he had taken from Cameron out of his pocket and laid it on the table, asking Cameron, "Did you notice anything peculiar about this note, other than the message?"

When he got no response, Peterson began unfolding the paper, and continued, "Notice how the note seemed to be folded haphazardly. But I want you to look closely at the pattern of the fold marks once I lay it flat on the table." Peterson might have been a magician revealing secrets to his apprentices.

The other two men peered intently at the paper, and Grainger spoke first: "Well, I'll be; I can make out the shape of a star."

"Excellent, deputy; you get the A-plus this time. I've intercepted one other message lost by a careless Level Two in Phoenix. I understand he disappeared without a trace too. Although the locations of the folds in his note differ slightly, they still form a star pattern. It's an effective and simple way to authenticate the note. A casual observer wouldn't think a thing about the way the note was folded. I doubt I would have caught it on the first note if the light hadn't hit it in a way that made the pattern more obvious. I was more intent on deciphering the written code on the paper. Raylene's clue verifies my suspicions about the star pattern."

"That's interesting but I still don't understand how they could talk someone like Raylene, who was basically honest, into helping them."

"Like I said, they lure people who need money. Sometimes money isn't necessary. For instance they might use blackmail, or appeal to patriotism, or lead someone to believe they're helping with a government sting. Whatever has the best effect on a given person, they'll use it."

"All right, I follow you so far, but why so much activity here in Fullwood County?"

"From the amount of movement I've seen here, coupled with other information I already have from other operatives, I believe your county is pivotal to something big that's about to happen. With your nuclear power plant, major seaport, and munitions terminal nearby, it wouldn't surprise me to find they're about to launch a coup, with Fullwood County as their primary staging point"

Both Cameron and Grainger were too stunned by the revelation to speak.

Peterson looked at his watch. "Listen, Cameron, it's time for you to be home. I've got one more important thing to tell you; otherwise any other questions have to wait."

Cameron's own watch read eleven-fifteen, and he told Peterson, "I think you're right. We've still got to get back to my truck."

"No worry about that," Peterson replied, "it's right out back. As I was taking you to my car, Deputy Grainger was getting your truck to bring it here. He used a shortcut."

Looking at Grainger, Cameron said, "I don't even want to know how he got it started without a key." Grainger just grinned sheepishly and looked at the floor.

Cameron looked back to Peterson and said, "I know you told me no more questions but I have to ask at least one more. Did you by any chance have anything to do with the DA's office dropping the investigation into Fishbait's death?"

"Yeah, don't be too hard on them, especially your friend Bill," responded Peterson. "They really wanted to pursue it, but I twisted their arms pretty hard. I couldn't give them any details, but I told them they would be hindering a Federal investigation."

"Well, that makes me feel a little better about my old classmate."

Peterson hesitated for a moment, then said, "After finding out how much Raylene trusted you, the only thing left to tell you—or ask you—right now is whether you're willing to be on my team?"

Cameron again was caught by surprise and just stared back at Peterson.

Peterson hurriedly added, "I can understand your reluctance. You'll be paid, although it can't be anything like your normal hourly rate, and you won't be on any official payroll. I also think that things are getting ready to happen very soon, so you won't be away from your practice too long. You will also be doing a favor to the President and your country."

Cameron laughingly replied, "If you hadn't mentioned the low pay, I'd swear you were giving me the same sales pitch you told me this group gives. You know I can't do this without my wife Mary knowing what's happening."

"I understand. I suspect you've already told her some of what's happened to you. In fact, it might be good to have her on guard inside the power plant. I think there's a Level Three or higher planted somewhere inside but I haven't been able to place an operative in there. It's up to you how much to tell her, so long as she understands the gravity of what's going on and only talks about the operation with you."

"Hell, I wouldn't be able to keep her from knowing something funky is going on, and she's probably in about as much danger as I am already. If she agrees, we're in."

"Good. I'm glad you understand that this will be a very dangerous undertaking. We'll have to give you code names, and clue you in on ours."

"You mean real, live, super-secret spy stuff?"

"You betcha. You've got a lot to learn, and almost no time to learn it; I'll have to teach you on the fly. I'll come to your office at nine tomorrow morning to confirm whether you and Mary are a go. Make that ten; I just remembered I need to meet with my Bureau personnel at nine. I'll give them the excuse that I have to ask you a few more questions. Meantime, be thinking of what to tell the people in your office about your upcoming absences. Tomorrow I'll also let you know where and when our next meeting will be."

"All right. So what are the code names?"

"I am 'Butterfly', and Deputy Grainger is 'Bee'. You and Mary will be... let's see... 'Diamond Jim' and 'Gravy Boat'."

"Now how in the world do you get those names from thinking about us?"

"That's the point; they have nothing to do with you. Those are the first things that popped into my head. We want nothing that will give someone a clue to your identities. The only ones who'll know who you are will be me, Deputy Grainger, and yourselves. For now, even my other operatives won't know you exist. Now let's all go and get some sleep. We have some busy days ahead."

Peterson doused the light after he and Grainger reattached their earpieces. A few minutes after Grainger slipped out the door into the darkness, Peterson said "OK" into his collar mike and then, placing a hand on Cameron's shoulder, guided him out the door and across the yard. Once they reached Cameron's hidden truck, Peterson disappeared into the darkness.

As Cameron pushed the start button on his keyring and stepped into the truck, he thought, *"I'm not sure which will be more dangerous; taking on the assignment, or telling Mary her codename is 'Gravy Boat'."*

CHAPTER TWENTY

During the drive home, Cameron's mind conjured shadowy assassins in every other car he passed. He wondered what he had gotten himself and Mary into, and ruminated on how paranoid he might become.

By the time he got home, Mary was in bed. She left a note propped on the entry table, asking him to wake her up when he got in.

Cameron gently shook Mary as he sat on the edge of the bed, and then spent the next hour-and-a-half relating the day's events to her. He carefully answered each of her many questions, reassured her that he would be as careful as he could under the circumstances, and promised to find answers to the things he did not yet know.

After a long, thoughtful pause, Mary agreed that they should help Peterson and told Cameron she had only one more question: "How do you get to be 'Diamond Jim' and I get stuck with 'Gravy Boat?'"

"I was afraid you'd ask that. I promise, it has nothing to do with us personally. Peterson's only seen you once but he doesn't even know you. He just knows he doesn't get me without you."

Only half mollified, Mary let the issue rest. She was too exhausted to argue the point anyway. Flinging the bed covers back, she said, "Come on and get in Diamond Jim, it's late and we've both got a big day tomorrow."

As he flopped into the bed and pulled the covers over both of them Cameron responded, "As you wish, Gravy Boat."

"You're lucky I'm too tired to smack you, Bubba."

They slept fitfully for what was left of the night.

~

When the radio blared next morning, Mary slammed the snooze button so hard it nearly knocked the radio off the table. She groggily rolled over to face Cameron and looked at him with one barely-opened eye. "Ooooh man," she moaned, "we really have to cut back on the party schedule."

Opening a bleary eye, Cameron looked back at her and said, "I had the strangest dream about somebody wanting us to be spies or something". He rolled on his back, squeezed both eyes shut and yawned.

Mary responded, "I had the strangest dream that some asshole called me Gravy Boat. Tell me that was just a nightmare."

"Sorry. You'll have to take that up with Gene."

"You bet I will. Meantime, we better get up, like it or not."

Mary gently patted Cameron on the thigh then stumbled out of the bed and into the bathroom. He stumbled right behind her. In the middle of brushing her teeth, Mary asked Cameron, "Did I understand correctly that this... group... essentially plans to start a revolution right here? In Riverport?"

"Well here or somewhere nearby."

"How are they planning to do that?"

Cameron turned off his electric razor mid-shave. "You know, I don't have the foggiest. Gene says he doesn't know enough yet to tell exactly what they plan to do. He just knows something's brewing."

"So I'm looking for something strange at the plant, but I don't know what and I don't know who?"

"That about sums it up. Anything else I can help you with?"

"No, no. Just wondering."

"Oh. Well... Good. Glad you now know as much as me." They both laughed and Cameron resumed his shaving as Mary finished brushing her teeth.

They lingered as long as possible over breakfast, confining their conversation to small-talk. At one point Mary set her coffee cup down, looked searchingly into Cameron's eyes and asked, "Are you sure we know what we're getting into?"

"Hell no. But if all this is as serious as it sounds, I don't think we have a choice."

"I guess you're right. It's just scary. I mean, this is our own government and we don't even know who to trust. Do we even know we can trust Gene Peterson?"

"Do we know we can trust him? No, I guess we don't know for sure. But I guess we have to for now."

She sighed resignedly and took another sip of coffee. Cameron rather mechanically finished the last of his breakfast cereal and started toward the door. Mary followed and at the door they stopped for a good bye hug and kiss. Brushing some imaginary specks of dust off his shoulders, Mary looked deep into Cameron's eyes and said, "Promise me you'll be extra careful. And call me if you find out anything I should know."

"I will be careful. I'll do my best about calling, but remember we're not sure whose phone is bugged and who might be listening in otherwise. I'll let you know something as soon as I can, the best way I can, OK?"

"OK. I love you."

"Love you too. You be careful yourself."

After one more lingering hug, they left for work.

Cameron arrived at his office at about eight-thirty and immediately called the staff together for a meeting. He told them, "I met somebody at a party a few weeks ago and they called me at home yesterday to set up a meeting at their place of business. It's, uh, well it's a very large commercial transaction and they're being very secretive right now. I'll be meeting at their place."

Nedra asked, "Should I just tell people you're at the court house?"

"Depends on who it is. Let Ben handle as much as possible. I'm sorry I can't tell any of you the details yet, but that's the way the client wants it. Of course once things get settled, I'm sure you'll all be working on the project. In the meantime, Ben is in charge." With a wry grin, Cameron added, "Which means, as Ben knows, that Nedra is in charge."

When the laughter settled, Cameron concluded, "This may take several days so I'll check in from time to time to be sure everything is all right. Just don't call me, unless it's Mary with an emergency. Shoot, you all know what to do and we've got enough backlog to keep everybody busy anyway. Any questions?"

Coleen, the real estate closing secretary, asked, "We've got quite a few closings coming up. What if there's too much new work for Ben to handle on top of everything else?"

"If it's not a regular client, refer them to Jimmy Humphrey or Bill Fairfax's office. They do good work and they refer a lot of people to us. If you're still not sure, wait until I check in. Anybody else?"

No one had any further questions. Cameron added, "One more thing. I'm expecting Mr. Peterson, the FBI agent, at ten. OK, let's get to work."

Everyone went to their respective workplaces, including Cameron, who stayed busy reviewing and signing documents until Peterson arrived. Nedra was polite to Peterson but not overly cordial. She had grown protective of her employer over the years and had no idea what kind of problems this FBI agent presented.

When Cameron came to the reception area he noticed Nedra's cool demeanor toward Peterson. For the moment he did nothing to discourage that attitude, preferring that the staff have no idea he was about to go to work for the man. He and Peterson greeted each other formally, using last names only, until safely behind the closed door of Cameron's office. They then resumed their conversation on a first-name basis.

Peterson began, "Well, what's the word, Cameron? Are you ready to be a 'G-man'?"

Cameron rejoined, "I believe 'I-man' would be more appropriate, Gene."

"I-man?"

"Uh-huh. For the Idiot I am, letting my curiosity get me into this."

Grinning and holding out his hand, Peterson said, "I had you figured right. I just knew you wouldn't let your country down."

Shaking Peterson's hand reluctantly, Cameron replied, "Just remember, if something happens to me I will come back and haunt you."

Peterson's response was a sardonic grin, and Cameron continued, "Where do we go from here? I still have no idea what we're really doing or looking for."

The agent replied, "I barely do myself. First, let me give you a communication device like the one you saw me using last night."

Peterson took the apparatus out of his pocket and showed Cameron how to wear the earpiece and microphone for optimum voice contact. He continued, "These are duplicates of the set I use overtly around my Bureau people and local law enforcement. The difference is; the ones we used last night, and yours, are much like cell phones that use a hard-to-scan digital signal. You'll only be able to use yours when you're sure you can't be seen wearing it. Put it in your car. When you get close to our meeting place tonight, just push the button I showed you and say my codename and nothing else. Don't come in until you hear me or Elliott say your codename, and the word 'no'."

"'No'?"

"It's actually the initials 'n' and 'o', for 'no obstruction', which means all clear."

Cameron nodded and said, "I see, the old backward logic ploy. When my buddies and I girl-watched as teenagers, we'd shake our heads and say 'no' whenever a good-looker came by. What it meant was, 'no, I wouldn't turn that one down'."

Peterson replied, "Sounds like typical teenage egos but yeah, that's pretty close. I like your twisted way of thinking though."

Cameron lamented, "That's all right, real life has dampened the ego quite a bit, and I suspect I'll need the twisted way of thinking for what I'm about to get into."

"Which is going to be quite a bit. I've got to go now but first here's where and when we'll meet next. You're familiar with Landler Road?"

Cameron nodded.

"Good. Elliott has found us another abandoned house there. I guess you know he has patrol duty as well as jail duty. He's got a pretty good inventory of potential meeting places he found while cruising. Turn right off of highway two-forty onto Landler, then go seven tenths of a mile. There'll be a dirt drive on the left. It won't be easy to spot, but look for a crumpled beer can next to a hubcap on the roadside. That's where you'll turn. If a car is in sight anywhere on the road don't slow down; just keep going and turn around when it's clear. OK so far?"

Cameron nodded again, and Peterson continued, "Once you're on the drive, use your communicator right away and wait for a response before you go any further. If you get no response, back out and go home and I'll get up with you later. Also, if you have any idea that someone may be following you, abandon the whole thing. Questions so far?"

"Yup. How far to the house once I'm in the driveway?"

"It'll only be about a hundred yards, but don't go to the house, go to the barn you'll see on the left. The big door will be open for you to drive in."

Cameron thought for a second, then said, "All right. What time?"

"Time yourself to be there at nine thirty. If you're more than five minutes late, we'll leave and contact you later. Tell Mary not to expect you home 'til at least two in the morning. Now, I really do have to go. See you tonight."

As Cameron escorted Peterson out of his office he said, loud enough for nearby staff to hear, "All right Mr. Peterson, I hope you find Steven Raeford's killer. If I think of anything else I'll let you know."

Peterson answered curtly, "Thank you Mr. Scott. And I'll call if I have any more questions."

In answer to Nedra's questioning look as Peterson left, Cameron said only, "He's still looking into Fishbait's death. At least he doesn't think I killed him."

Not convinced, she asked, "What if he comes back while you're gone?"

Cameron answered, "Don't worry, I really don't think he'll have any more questions."

The statement was true. From now on Cameron would have all the questions. Telling Nedra, "I'll be in touch," he went out the door and climbed into his truck.

CHAPTER TWENTY-ONE

By the time Cameron and Peterson finished their conversation it was nearly eleven-thirty. Cameron decided on an early lunch at "The Lonely Oyster", the restaurant where Raylene had worked. He glanced furtively up and down the street on the way to his pickup, then slid in and quickly locked the communicator in the glove box. While driving, he thought, "*Wonder how long it took Peterson to quit feeling like everybody's out to get him. I'll have to ask next time I see him.*" He switched the radio on for company, keeping a close watch in the rearview mirror until he reached the restaurant.

Cameron climbed the few stairs to the restaurant's front porch and plunked a couple of quarters into the vending box by the door for a daily paper. Then he went in and settled into a corner booth. From this relatively secure perch he surveyed the eclectic mix of college banners, seascapes and sports pictures that passed for the restaurant's décor before scanning the sparse group of patrons. He chose The Lonely Oyster for lunch mostly because tourists did not. It was fairly small and out of the way, frequented most often by locals.

As he nodded 'hello' to several people, Cameron thought, "*This is good; at least I recognize everybody in here by face if not by name. Maybe I can relax for a while.*"

He unfolded the paper and laid it on the table then took the cell phone from his pocket and pushed the speed dial for Mary's work number. It took her a while to come to the phone, and when she did he said, "Hey, it's me. What took so long?"

She answered, "Oh, I've had to get some glitches out of the computer system. Something's not quite right but I think I've about got it fixed. Nothing that'll trigger an automatic shutdown though. What's up?"

"I've got an 'appointment' tonight, so I'll be late getting home."

She let him know she understood by answering, "OK, I'll leave the light on for you" without asking any more questions.

He continued, "Talk to you when I get home if not before. Hope you get everything fixed all right. Love you."

"Love you too. I might be a little late myself, but I think we got this thing figured out. We've got a couple of new people and they're not used to our system I guess. Bye bye."

By the time the call was over, the waitress was at the table so he ordered a cheeseburger with fries and a drink before settling in to read the paper. The day's headlines included the usual life and strife in the nearby city of Whittington; 'Man Arrested After Midtown Car Chase', 'City Counsel To Look At Roads', 'Mayor Looks At Annexation Problem'. *"Seems like they do a lot of looking and not much doing up there"* thought Cameron.

Soon, a front-page recap of the hurricane season caught Cameron's eye. *"Although hurricanes have spared the coastal area around Whittington and Riverport so far this year"* it read, *"weather experts fear that Hurricane Mary will not be so kind."* The story went on with the usual cautions about stocking batteries and water, and having plywood ready to cover windows. A tracking map printed under the story projected Mary making landfall anywhere from Charleston to Virginia Beach, with Riverport about in the middle. According to the accompanying story, landfall would be in about five days. Cameron was glad he finally remembered to buy batteries. Now if he could remember the bottled water.

After dawdling over lunch and the paper for about an hour and a half, Cameron decided to go back to the cabin and wait for the night's excursion. He ordered a ham sandwich to go and picked out a couple of canned drinks from the refrigerated case near the checkout. On the way to the cabin he recalled that the transponder was still attached to his truck and wondered if anyone was tracking his whereabouts at the moment.

The driveway to the cabin was still overgrown, so Cameron did his usual U-turn and parked across the road. On approaching the footpath he thought, *"I've used this path so much lately I could probably take it blindfolded."* That thought quickly faded as he ducked under the branches where the path bisected the swamp.

Before he could straighten to continue walking he saw movement ahead. A short distance in front of him a ten-foot alligator lumbered across the path, intent on finding its way into the murky waters on the other side. Not wanting to draw the beast's attention, Cameron remained crouched and motionless until the 'gator glided into the swamp. He stepped gingerly for the rest of the hike to the cabin.

At the cabin, Cameron switched on the main power, put the sandwich and drinks into the refrigerator, and meandered to the front porch to settle into a rocker. The cabin's location on a high bluff afforded him a spectacular view that extended past the intracoastal waterway and adjacent barrier island community of Crescent Beach to the ocean.

Fortunately, Crescent Beach had strict ordinances to prevent high-rise structures from blocking the vista. It also had one of the few south-facing beaches on the east coast, which allowed its residents and visitors to enjoy both ocean sunrises and ocean sunsets.

As Cameron rocked, he closed his eyes and breathed deeply, trying to take his mind off the jumble of disturbing information that had been thrown at him. The sounds and smells of the waterside retreat soon flooded his senses. Hints of salt air mingled with the scent of freshwater streams that mixed with the musty smell of freshly plowed dirt in nearby fields. Squalling gulls accented the steady drone of motorboats that underscored the lap of water against the shore.

Suddenly the lulling symphony was rudely interrupted by a loud buzz. It sounded frighteningly like the hornets from his nightmare. Jolted from his reverie, Cameron blinked his eyes a few times against the bright sun and looked for the source of the sound. Seeing that it was a pair of jet-skis speeding past, he breathed a sigh of relief.

Since he was now wide awake, Cameron began idly scanning the distant horizon. He could make out the shapes of two ships, one heading toward the river inlet and one that appeared to be sitting still. Although ships often idled just off the coast awaiting pilots to guide them into and up the river, few of them anchored while waiting. He could not tell if this one was anchored, but wondered if it was the ship that was having trouble.

Cameron recalled an article in today's paper that followed up the earlier report about the ship with engine trouble. The story read, *"The main engine did not fail, as earlier reported, but the electric motor that operates the rudder has malfunctioned. A spokesman for the*

85

shipping line said the ship's mechanic is expecting repair parts any time now, and expressed his concern about the delay in unloading."

So he could take a closer look at the ship, Cameron stepped back inside, grabbed the small brass telescope that stood near a front window, and brought it onto the porch. He also brought one of the references that was kept near the telescope to identify birds, ships and anything else that might pass at a distance.

He set the telescope on its tripod at the edge of the porch, training its lens on the ship. According to the reference book, the ship was a freighter; a type known as a ro-ro, short for roll-on, roll-off. Some freight containers were stacked on the exposed upper deck, and it had the distinctive stern ramp common to that class of ro-ro. The ramp would be lowered to the wharf so containers could be driven out of the lower freight decks. He could also see an anchor chain extending from the ship's bow into the water, making it more likely that it was the one with problems.

Cameron saw nothing else on the horizon, so he settled back into the rocker and called his office. Nedra answered and immediately asked, "Is everything going all right?"

Cameron answered, "Everything's fine here. We've gone into heavy negotiations but I'm getting a chance to come up for air."

Nedra queried, "Where are you? Sounds like seagulls in the background."

"Oh, I've stepped outside for a little bit. I'm at the south end of the county, right at the waterfront. Ben having any problems?"

Although she covered the phone with her hand, Cameron could still hear Nedra holler to Ben in the back of the building before she came back on and responded, "No, he says he's got it all under control."

Cameron stifled a laugh and said, "Well, good." To keep up the pretense about the commercial land deal negotiations he added, "Listen, tell Ben I need him to update the Swenson and Jaskowicz title files. Can't say why, but I may need them for this deal. Otherwise, I'll check back in tomorrow."

After Nedra said "Good bye" and hung up, Cameron tried once again to relax but found it impossible. His mind kept springing back to the mysterious organization and why it was so interested in Fullwood County. Realizing that he knew too little yet to form any answers, he went inside, pulled a well-read cartoon book off a shelf and went back out to the Porch. The rocker, the book and the cool breeze worked; he soon dozed off.

The noise of a passing motorboat woke Cameron at around five. The nap was just long enough for him to feel refreshed but not groggy. After a stretch and a yawn, he stepped inside to retrieve the sandwich and a soft drink, and took them to the kitchen table for supper. As he ate, it occurred to him that he should probably prepare the cabin for the approaching storm. Since the cabin was built with hurricanes in mind, it would not take long.

After he ate, Cameron lugged the storm shutters from under the cabin and latched them all into place over the windows. Next he walked down the long slope to the dockside rack and unfastened the canoe to carry it to the cabin. He rolled it upright and used both hands to grasp the wooden thwarts that spanned side to side, and hoisted it until it rested lengthwise on his hip.

Walking sideways, Cameron slowly hauled the canoe up the hill, set it on a rack built for it beside the cabin and tied it down. He sat down for a few minutes to catch his breath before taking two more trips to retrieve the paddles, trolling motor, and other gear from a dockside bin to store inside the cabin. There was not much he could do about the dock itself; any significant storm surge would carry it away.

When he finished all the storm preparations, Cameron saw that it was time to leave for his meeting with Peterson. In the waning daylight, he locked the door and switched off the main power before retracing his route back to the truck, carefully looking for alligators before crossing the swamp again.

Cameron had worked up a sweat preparing the cabin in the August heat and humidity, so he used his remote starter as soon as the pickup was in sight. He knew the air conditioner was on and he wanted to get it running while he did an inspection. The best he could tell, the truck was untouched. No new tire tracks were apparent on the road or roadside, nor were there signs that any had been obliterated. He looked under the vehicle this time, spotting the transponder where Elliott placed it but nothing else out of the ordinary. Satisfied that it was safe to go, Cameron climbed in and headed toward his rendezvous.

CHAPTER TWENTY-TWO

Cameron retrieved a county roadmap and the communicator from the glove compartment as he started his trip into the countryside. He calculated the time it would take to reach Landler Road and adjusted his speed accordingly. At precisely nine-thirty he spied the crushed can and hubcap in the location described by Peterson and made his turn. The driveway was barely discernible after years of neglect but once his headlights shined on it, he could tell another car had passed earlier.

As soon as he was off the road, Cameron said "Butterfly" into the communicator. He thought he recognized Elliott's voice when the "no" response came a few seconds later. Taking one more look up and down Landler Road he plunged the truck through the tangle of weeds, traveling slowly until he spied a dilapidated barn with open doors to his left. He cautiously pulled into the barn and parked behind a sheriff's cruiser. Although no one was in sight, he saw the doors swing shut behind him before he turned off his headlights.

Then there was nothing but silence and darkness. Cameron nearly jumped out of his seat when a beam of light suddenly glared through the the window at his side. Elliott's voice cut through the darkness, "Sorry Mr. Scott, we still had to make sure it was you. Come on out."

Cameron stepped out onto the straw-littered dirt that passed for a floor. Although the barn looked as though it had been abandoned for some time, he could still detect a faint pungent smell of livestock.

Elliott slipped his service revolver back into its holster and motioned for Cameron to follow him into a small enclosure that appeared to be a feed or tack room. In it, three chairs sat around a rough work table on which sat a small battery-operated lamp. Peterson was already seated and when he nodded toward the other chairs, Cameron and Elliott took their places at the table. Cameron noticed that Peterson was also reholstering a pistol.

After the men exchanged brief greetings, Peterson continued his narrative from the night before. "I know you're anxious to find out what's going on, so I'll get right to it" he said.

Peterson settled into his chair and continued, "As I told you last night, the little group of eggheads that wanted to make some quiet changes from within the government was quickly taken over by folks who weren't so patient. It seems like every organization gets a few like them, but they're usually not quite so dangerous. You know the type; they think they have all the answers and don't want to wait their turn to lead, so they just try to take over. Sometimes it works, especially if the original leaders would rather avoid confrontation. Usually it's volunteer groups. Sometimes they get their mission changed, sometimes they just fold from within, but there's not much harm to the general public."

Cameron interjected, "I've seen it happen a few times. And you're right; a lot of people who do volunteer work do it for the enjoyment, and don't want the headache of power struggles. They'd rather put their time into something more rewarding."

"Exactly. But like I said, the potential for disaster is huge with this group. First they're embedded in almost every part of our government but they're insidious. If you tried to warn the public about them you'd be put off as a paranoid lunatic, assuming you didn't just disappear first. Second, they're ruthless; they have no qualms about getting people out of their way. Third, I'm not altogether certain how far they've spread by now. I just know they've got to be stopped." Cameron thought he saw a hint of fear in Peterson's eyes, but only for a second.

Cameron asked, "Are they right-wingers or left-wingers, or what?"

Peterson answered, "Both and neither. You can't really put a label on them. The common denominator seems to be a hatred for the current political system. They have the twisted idea that the only way to save democracy now is to destroy it first and start over. Of course they'll be the ones dispensing 'democracy' once they gain power."

"Do they not realize how our defenses would be undermined, how vulnerable we would become?"

"Remember, they think they have all the answers. And that type of ego blinds itself to anything that might contradict those answers. I'm sure they think their collective wisdom will overcome all."

"Have they gotten a foothold in our military?"

"That's the saving grace so far. I think they've tested the waters and found them pretty cold in the military branches. In this case it's fortunate that our military brass are pretty dedicated to maintaining the status quo. In fact two of my good contacts among that brass were fellow chopper pilots in 'Nam, and they haven't seen any unusual activity. But from what I can tell about these folks, they have the ego to think the military will just fall in once the grand plan is revealed."

"So it's us against the bureaucrats."

"I won't lump all government folk into one category here. Remember, these are renegade egomaniacs who think their time has come, not your typical career nine-to-fivers."

"So what happens now and what can Mary and I do?"

Peterson took a deep breath and studied the tabletop for a moment before answering. "I think the group is about to make a significant move toward their goal, and I think it's going to start right here in 'River City'."

Cameron's eyes widened. "You're kidding. Here?"

"You betcha. There's been far too much activity around here with their mark on it and all the killings lead me to believe something big is going down. I think your erstwhile client put a temporary kink in the plans, but only temporary. I wish I could figure out what message he was supposed to deliver and where he hid it."

"You don't think the message was verbal?"

"No, they wouldn't have trusted him to get it straight. And they wouldn't have let him know the message in the first place. I think it was on him somewhere. Nothing was found on or in his body during the autopsy, so it must have been in something he wore or carried."

Cameron turned to Elliott and asked, "Didn't you tell me Fishbait's possessions went out with his body?"

Elliott nodded, adding, "I did say that and it was the truth, but I couldn't tell you before that everything went straight to Mr. Peterson."

Cameron turned back to Peterson and said simply, "Well?"

Peterson replied, "This is the first I've had enough time and security to take them out for examination. I didn't dare send them to the lab." He lifted a canvas duffel off the floor and set it on the table. Dumping out its contents, he said, "Let's see what we can figure out."

For a few moments they stared at the few belongings on the table: a pair of faded jeans, a stained tee shirt, underwear, a pair of short white fisherman's boots, a few coins, and a well-used pocketknife. One by one the items received closer inspection. Peterson turned the jeans, underwear and tee shirt inside out and held them to the light; Elliott ripped open seams; Cameron disassembled the pocketknife and tore into the boots. Nothing was out of the ordinary.

When they were done, all three silently slouched in their chairs, wondering how they could make the inanimate objects reveal their secret. Cameron languidly pushed one of the coins, a nickel, around the table with one finger, watching shadows shift on the relief of Monticello as it neared the table lamp. He let out a bemused chuckle as he focused on the rotunda of the building.

Peterson asked, "What could you find funny at this point?"

Cameron replied, "I was just thinking about how many thousands of nickels I've probably handled in my lifetime, and never noticed this one detail."

What detail?"

"Well, it looks like there's something engraved on Monticello's rotunda. I can tell there's something there, but I can't quite make it out."

Peterson was galvanized. "Holy crap, that's it!"

"What's it?"

"The message. Let me see that coin." Peterson snatched the coin to his side of the table, and pulled the light close to it. He reached to the floor again, picked up a briefcase, and retrieved a small round magnifying glass from it. As he peered through the glass, he told Elliott to take out a pen and paper. "I know damn well there's not supposed to be anything engraved on that dome. Write this down, Elliott— the capital letters 'H, S, S' and a plus sign with the number '8' next to it. I'll give those s.o.b.s credit; they know how to play the game."

"What are you talking about?"

"They had a message etched on the coin. Think of the beauty of it. Steven, or 'Fishbait' as you knew him, is given a coin and told to drop it in the middle of the night at his destination point, probably a pay phone or vending machine. He doesn't even have to know he's a messenger. After he leaves, the intended recipient breaks into the machine and removes all the nickels, takes them to a safe place, and finds the one with the message. The etching is large enough that you noticed it under the strong light, but it's minute enough that nobody else would normally take note of it, just in case anything went wrong."

"So what does it mean?"

"That's the next question to work on. But I can't tell you how much you've earned your keep already, Cameron. You seem to have a knack for noticing details."

"I suspect it's more luck than knack but I'm glad it helped."

"Don't downplay it too much, no matter how you did it. This is a major breakthrough, figuring out another part of their messaging system. Now let's see if we can decode what little they gave us to work with." They pulled their chairs up to the table and leaned over the paper on which Elliott had written the cryptic symbols.

CHAPTER TWENTY-THREE

"H S S plus eight; I don't get it," mused Elliott. "What kind of message could that be to anybody?"

"Beats me," said Cameron.

Peterson, brow furrowed, concentrated for a few moments, then sighed and said, "Let's talk out loud a little bit. Most likely the letters are somebody's initials, but let's not get hung up on just that. If you think of somebody or something that has those letters, speak up. You might have the answer, or you might spark something in one of us that will give us the answer. I don't think they would use the initials of any group member though, since they take so many precautions to conceal their identities. Is there a store or something around here whose name uses those letters? Maybe it has something to do with a meeting place."

Cameron and Elliott looked at each other and shrugged but neither had an immediate answer. Then Cameron said, "The only kind of place I can think of is 'high school shop.' Would they want to meet at a school wood shop for some reason?"

"I wouldn't rule out anything at this point," replied Peterson, "but let's keep going."

Cameron and Elliott kept tossing out ideas, some serious, and some a little lighter, such as "have some soup" and "high seas skullduggery", but Peterson seemed preoccupied. Suddenly, he slammed his hand down on the table and exclaimed, "Whoa, wait, wait, that's it! I told you we might spark something in each other. Cameron, when you said 'high seas skullduggery', something clicked in the back of my mind that wouldn't go away, then it came to me."

In unison, Cameron and Elliott asked, "What?"

"It was the words 'high seas' that did it. There's a reason they used capital letters. Did you happen to read about the ship that's been waiting for parts?"

Cameron answered, "Yeah."

"The papers never said what the ship was called" continued Peterson, "but I checked out the reports the Coast Guard made after their inspection of the ship, looking for anything unusual. Nothing looked out of the ordinary but I remember laughing at the name of the ship. It's owned by the High Sea lines. The owner must be an opera fan or terrible punster, because he named this one the 'High Sea Soprano'."

Peterson's revelation was greeted with blank stares, followed by a groan from Cameron.

Still perplexed, Elliott said, "I don't get it. What's the pun?"

Cameron answered, "Think of music notes. You know, A, B, C. High C is pretty far up on the scale for the human voice. Usually takes a good tenor or soprano to reach it."

"Oh, OK, I get it now. So, Mr. Peterson, you think the letters have something to do with that ship?"

"I'm just about positive. The group must have a Level Three operative in the Coast Guard that made sure the inspection didn't amount to much. I guess I need to warn my pentagon contacts to watch out after all; looks like they're getting a foothold in the military That ship must have something to do with whatever the group is up to. I've got to check it out closer."

"All right, but what about the 'plus eight?" asked Elliott.

"I've been thinking about that," said Cameron, "and I have an idea."

"Let's hear it," said Peterson.

"All right. Gene, you said you think something is imminent, right? What if the eight means eight hours or eight days? The plus sign could mean that something will happen in that amount of time."

Peterson said, "Sounds logical but eight days is more likely. Eight hours from whenever they would've gotten the message wouldn't be much time to organize anything. But eight days from when?"

"From the day Fishbait was supposed to deliver the message, which technically was Monday morning, so I'd say count Tuesday as day one."

As Cameron mentally counted the days, he could tell from the looks on the other two men's faces that each of them had the same sinking feeling. Elliott spoke first. "Today would be the eighth day, wouldn't it? Maybe it don't mean eight days, because the day's about over and nothing's happened."

"No, wait," interrupted Peterson, "the message didn't get delivered on time, so there might have been some delay in plans. I'm sure they got another Level One messenger once they learned about Steven's arrest, but some step in the process must have depended on his message being delivered that night. We sure as hell can't waste any more time though. I've got to figure out a way onto that ship."

After putting the magnifying glass back into his briefcase, Peterson unholstered his pistol to inspect it then turned to Cameron and said, "I never asked you if you had any firearms. Do you?"

"Not any more. In my ranger days, I carried a small service revolver, but never had to use it. Our wildlife was too civilized, and the worst crime our visitors usually committed was littering. When I went to law school, I gave it to my cousin who works with Fish and Wildlife."

"Try to get hold of another one. You might need it."

"I'll check with my friend Larry. I think he keeps a small arsenal in his house."

Peterson related his plan to Cameron and Elliott. "I mostly need you two to be my eyes and ears. Cameron, Mary needs to let you know if she sees anything the least bit out of sync with routine at the plant. You know how to get in touch with me. If I don't respond right away, wait at least fifteen minutes before you try again. Keep the chatter short and sweet. If you need to tell me a lot of detail, let Elliott know. I don't have time to teach you our meeting-place codes but Elliott knows them. I can tell him where to meet, and he can get you where you need to go."

Cameron said, "OK so far."

Peterson continued, "I want you to be extra careful, Cameron. You'll need to be a little paranoid because I'm not sure I was the only one intercepting some of your phone calls. In fact, try to keep all your conversations with Mary face to face." Turning to Elliott, he said, "Keep in touch with our usual contacts. I also want you to see if our man at the munitions depot has seen anything suspicious, and put him on alert."

Cameron said accusingly, "I thought you didn't know who you could trust?"

"I don't, in the general population. My contacts up to this point are all people I've known, trusted, and relied on for a long time. You're the exception, but believe me; I've checked you and Mary out so thoroughly that I probably know you better than you do."

"I'm not sure if that doesn't scare me more than the unknown element out there."

"I hate to say it, but the report on you was actually pretty boring. Do you never misbehave?"

"Evidently you didn't ask Mary anything about me. According to her, I never behave."

"I'll look into that later. Meanwhile, here's what I want you to do tomorrow. Elliott, do you still have inmates that were in your jail while Steven was there?"

Elliott responded, "There's only been one or two released since then."

"Good. I want you to talk to as many as you can and see if Steven gave anybody an idea of where he was headed that night. Try to be a discreet as you can. Cameron, make sure Mary is up to speed on everything and get her to be especially careful of her co-workers. I can't help but think that some part of the group's grand plan includes the nuclear plant. Then try to get some sleep. I don't have anything specific for you to do tonight but I want you to be ready for anything tomorrow."

Cameron asked, "You don't think they'll start doing anything before then?"

Peterson answered, "No, I don't. I think Steven's little snack foray caused them at least a day's worth of replanning. I imagine they didn't think anything would go wrong with that simple phase of the operation, so they probably had to regroup after it got screwed up. I do want you to spend some time cruising around town tomorrow looking for any unusual activity."

"Such as…?"

"I'm not really sure. I know this is a tourist area, so you're used to having lots of strangers around. All I can tell you is, look for things that seem out of place."

"I think I understand" said Cameron.

Peterson concluded, "All right let's get out of here. You both know how to get in touch. Elliott and Cameron, I want you to check in with each other as soon as possible tomorrow. Cameron, wear your communicator any time you're alone. Elliott, you already know when you can use yours. Keep it short and sweet and if you need to, meet face to face. Have your first face-to-face at... where Cameron?"

Cameron replied, "Let's make it the Hardees right outside town."

"Hardees it is. After that, decide on each meeting place before you leave. I'll try to contact you whenever I can but I don't know how hard that may be if I get out to the ship. All right, that's all for now. Good night, gentlemen."

Peterson repacked the duffel and threw it to Elliott. Then he grabbed his briefcase with one hand and picked up the light with the other, using the lamplight to guide Cameron and Elliott back to the cars. Peterson told Cameron, "go ahead and put on your communicator now" and helped him put it on properly. All three men shook hands with each other and after Cameron and Elliott climbed into their cars, Peterson opened the barn doors for them to back out.

As Cameron started backing out of the barn, he heard Elliott's voice on the communicator, "Let me go out first. Nobody'll wonder that much why a patrol car is checking out some deserted property. I'll give the all clear."

Cameron asked, "Hasn't your office missed you by now?"

"Nah, I'm off duty."

Saying, "Oh", Cameron backed out and turned his car to face the drive, leaving room for Elliott.

Elliott backed out of the barn next and turned to go out the drive. After closing the barn doors, Peterson climbed into the patrol car and they headed toward the road. Cameron waited until he got the all clear before he started down the drive. When he reached the main road he could see the patrol car a short distance away on the roadside with its lights off.

Cameron took a circuitous route home, checking his rearview mirrors obsessively all the way. A few times he felt like he was being followed but the cars eventually turned other directions. When he finally pulled into his own drive he heard Peterson's voice in the communicator earpiece saying, "Good night Diamond Jim, sleep tight." No cars were in sight so he wondered how Peterson knew he was home. Then he remembered; the transponder was still signaling his location.

CHAPTER TWENTY-FOUR

By the time Cameron got home and caught Mary up to speed on the day's events, it was nearly 3:00 a.m.. Fortunately, Mary's shift that day did not start until noon, so they were able to get a few hours' sleep.

After seeing Mary off at eleven-thirty, Cameron donned the communicator. He called for "Butterfly" a few times, but was answered instead by "Bee". Elliott said, "I got some new information we need to talk about. Meet me at two o'clock."

Cameron, keeping it short and sweet, merely said, "OK" and there was no further conversation.

Next, Cameron called Larry's house to see about borrowing a firearm. Sandy answered on the first ring.

Cameron said, "Sandy, this is Cameron, is Larry in?"

Sounding a little shaky, Sandy responded, "No, he's not."

"I need to borrow one of his pistols... are you OK?"

With a slight tremble in her voice, she said, "No, I'm... Something's not right, Cameron. Larry piloted a ship up to Whittington this morning, and I haven't heard from him since he left the house about five."

Cameron knew that Larry always contacted Sandy after he got a ship piloted into port, so he asked, "He didn't leave a note or something?"

"No, I've looked in all the places he would have left one and called some of his friends and the Pilot's Association office, but nobody's seen him. I was about to call the port in Whittington when you called."

"Tell you what; stay put and I'll be right over. Meantime, make a few more calls and get me on my cell phone if you find anything out."

"I probably shouldn't be this worried, but it's not like him to wait this long to call."

Cameron said, "Maybe he just forgot to tell you and thought he did. I'll be there shortly. Take care."

Although he had tried to sound calm and reassuring to Sandy, Cameron's mind was racing from the minute she told him Larry was missing. He needed time to see Sandy but wanted Elliott to know there was a new development, and again called for "Bee". Elliott came on immediately.

"Bee, we've got something new," Cameron began. "Can't say why right now, but can you move our meeting up to 2:30?"

"No problem. I'm supposed to go out on the road at 3:00, though, so we can't take long."

"Are you pulling a double today?"

"Got to; we've got somebody out sick today."

"All right, see you at 2:30, and I'll fill you in after I find out more."

Cameron then headed straight for Larry's house, where Sandy invited him inside. Her eyes were red, but she appeared more composed, saying, "I'm probably being a big idiot about this, but he's always so good about letting me know where he'll be. He knows what a worry-wart I am after... you know. He can be aggravating as hell sometimes, but that's one thing he always does for me." Sandy's first husband had been found dead three days after he crashed into an overgrown ravine, and Cameron knew how worried she was now.

Cameron tried to sound as nonchalant as he could, saying, "Listen, I think he's fine. Did you get hold of anybody at the port?"

"I did, and they said somebody saw him get off the ship but nobody noticed which way he went. Like you said, he's probably fine. I just feel a little uneasy after reading in the paper what happened to Fishbait and his sister."

"Well, I understand that. I'm sure you've tried his cell phone."

"I've just been getting his voice mail. But that's not unusual when he goes up to the port. Sometimes the reception for his phone is awful up there. You know what, he's probably just waiting to take another ship out. If I don't hear from him in a couple more hours, I'll get back in touch with you."

"That's a good idea. In fact give me a call even if you do hear from him, so I'll know not to worry."

"OK thanks Cameron. I do feel a little better."

Cameron wished he did.

She continued, "Did you say something about borrowing one of Larry's pistols?"

"Oh, yes. I uh… I want to clear out some rattlers that took up residence under the cabin. If you could find me one with a full clip with it, I'd appreciate it."

"Larry was just cleaning them the other day after some target practice so I know he's got a couple ready to use. I'll see what I can find."

When Sandy left, Cameron quickly scanned the room for any sign of where Larry might have gone but found nothing. Soon she returned with a Glock 29 loaded with a ten-round clip. "This is the first one I came to," she said, "I hope it'll work for you."

"It's perfect, thanks. I'll take good care of it."

"Here's some extra clips, too"

"As always, you think of everything. It's been a while, so I might just miss on the first ten anyway. Thanks again."

Sandy grinned at the suggestion that Cameron might miss hitting the rattlers. Cameron often accompanied Larry and Sandy to the firing range to stay in practice, using Larry's firearms, and rarely missed the bullseye. Sandy was a good shot in her own right and Larry was the worst of them.

After giving Sandy a quick hug, Cameron hurried to the car for his meeting with Elliott. He locked the pistol in the glove compartment where he had left the communicator and headed straight for the restaurant. On the way, he stopped at a pay phone and made a quick call to Mary. When she came on, he said, "I'm about to get some new information. Tell you about it later. Anything new on your end?"

"A few odd things here and there, but nothing I can put my finger on yet."

"OK. Take care Babe. Love you."

"Me too. Bye." Cameron surmised that some of her co-workers must be nearby. He hung up and hurried to his meeting with Elliott.

At Hardees, Elliott was already seated at an isolated table and Cameron joined him. There were few other people in the restaurant.

Elliott spoke first. "I got us both cheeseburgers and Coke. Hope you don't mind but we don't have much time."

Cameron said, "Cheeseburger and Coke is perfect. What's up?"

As they began eating, Elliott continued, "I got some information on where Fishbait was headed that's gonna blow your mind."

"Where was he going?"

"Noplace."

"What?"

"He was already there."

"Elliott, quit talking in riddles."

"Sorry, I just thought it was kinda funny. What I mean is; the store where he was caught is where he was supposed to end up."

"I'll be damned. But there are a couple of drink machines and a pay phone outside that store, so it makes sense for the drop place. Looks like Fisbait got hungry before he made the drop and screwed up the plans. How'd you get that information?"

"Well, none of the inmates knew anything so I called the store owner to see if I could get any more information. He says he got a little antsy after they took Fishbait off and spent the rest of the night inside the store with the lights out and a shotgun in hand. About four in the morning he hears a car pull up in front and somebody gets out. He's ready to blast him if he comes in, but says the guy just goes up to one of the machines and buys a drink. The drinks are a buck apiece, and the guy uses a dollar bill, but get this— he checks the coin return anyway."

"Whoa. And finds nothing."

"Damn straight. Store owner says the guy went to the other drink machine and checked that coin return, and even checked out the pay phone, then started cussing a blue streak. The store owner figured the guy was just a cheapskate."

"So instead of breaking into the machine and sorting through a bunch of coins, he only had to look for one that Fishbait was supposed to drop in the coin-return. They banked on no one else using the machine in those early-morning hours. Could the store owner identify him?"

"He said it was too dark to tell who it was but he got the make of the car, and was able to catch some of the license plate when it passed under the parking lot security light. I got hold of Mr. Peterson before he left here and he's got somebody checking to see if they can pin down who owns the car with what they have. They're supposed to contact me if they get anywhere."

"Speaking of Gene, where is he? I haven't been able to get up with him."

"I got him early this morning before he left. He said he probably wouldn't be able to talk direct with either of us for a while. So tell me about your news."

"Yes, my news. Looks like my river pilot friend is missing. That really worries me with our mystery ship sitting out there."

"You talking about Larry Gullege?"

"Yup. I think you go hunting with him sometimes, don't you? Anyway, he's almost fanatical about letting Sandy know where he is. You remember how her first husband died? After it took so long for them to find him, she gets in a panic if Larry's even a half-hour late getting home. He took a ship upriver early this morning, and she hasn't heard from him since."

"No note or anything? I guess she's called everywhere she can think of?"

"She's done everything she could. I've tried to make her feel like everything's all right but I'm not sure I was too convincing. As soon as we're done here I'm going to call a few people I know at the port to see if they know anything."

Looking at his watch, Elliott said, "I gotta start my patrol. Keep in touch, and I'll let you know if I hear anything about that license plate they're checking. How about the 'Gas Hog' for the next meeting?" Cameron agreed.

As they started toward the door, Cameron noticed that some workmen were distributing plywood sheets around the perimeter of the building. He looked questioningly at Elliott.

Elliott, laughing, said, "Man, you gotta keep up. That hurricane's up to category four and they're pretty sure it's going to hit anywhere from below Myrtle Beach up to the southern Outer Banks. We're right in the middle. It's picking up forward speed too, something like twenty miles an hour toward the northwest now. It's probably going to hit sooner than they expected."

Cameron realized he was concentrating on the unfolding mystery so hard he neglected to keep up with the news. He wondered if the shadowy group would try to move faster or would put their plans on hold for the hurricane. He knew that either way, there was no time to lose.

CHAPTER TWENTY-FIVE

Cameron still needed to get a few chores done before dark, such as picking up bottled water and some other groceries. He decided that he could do that and check things out around town at the same time. But first he called his office to see if there were any problems.

Nedra answered and told him "things are pretty quiet, but some car drove by the office three times this afternoon going real slow." Since the office was a restored old house and in the middle of a side street, clients sometimes went by at least once before realizing where it was. She continued, "I know a lot of people miss us the first time, but three times without stopping seemed a bit odd to us."

Cameron thought so too, but said to Nedra, "I wouldn't worry about it, they're probably lost tourists. What kind of car was it?"

"It was some kind of dark green SUV, fairly new looking. It had Virginia tags on the front and back, but I didn't take down the numbers."

"Well , like I said, it probably was tourists." In case some of the staff might see him roaming around town, Cameron added, "Listen, I'll be checking out a few properties around town for the new client. There's some discrepancies in descriptions we need to straighten out. You probably already know more than me about the hurricane that's supposed to be coming; I've been so busy I just found out a little while ago. Go ahead and batten down the hatches at the office, then tell everyone to go home early and get their own houses ready." When he hung up, Cameron made a mental note get his home ready as well. Then he continued his journey around town.

On his way to his first stop, the mini-mart, Cameron called his contact at the state port; a former client whom he had helped in a boundary dispute.

When the man came to the phone, Cameron said, "Hey Sid, this is Cameron Scott. I need to ask you a favor. You know Larry Gullege? Do you have any idea where he went after he parked the ship he brought in today?"

"I'm sorry Cameron, I wasn't on duty when Larry brought it in. Is something wrong?"

"I doubt it, but Sandy hasn't heard from him in a while and you know how much she worries. I told her I'd check with you."

"Well, I haven't seen him at all but I'll check around. Want me to call if I find out anything?"

"That'll be great, Sid. Thanks. Talk to you later."

By this time Cameron was at the mini-mart, where he bought some cases of bottled water, more batteries and some extra flashlights. Next he headed toward some seldom traveled back streets and donned his communicator. One call to "Bee" was answered quickly. Cameron asked, "You remember the car we talked about, the one that came while the store owner was guarding his place? Did you say he got the a make of the car?"

Elliott responded, "ten-four; he said it was a dark green Explorer, looked new."

"Any luck with an ID on the tag?"

"Not yet."

"You might want to have them check Virginia. Don't want to say too much more right now."

"Will do. Anything else?"

"Nope. Pretty quiet otherwise."

They both signed off and Cameron headed for his next stop; an electronics store where Mary's laptop computer was being repaired. No one else was in the store, so Cameron began a conversation with the shopkeeper as he paid. "I understand we're the most likely target for the hurricane," he said, "That always keeps the tourists away."

The shopkeeper laughed and said, "Well most of them. Some'll come just to see what it's like to be in a hurricane, you know."

"That's true. I don't think many come back for a second look though. About the only scarier thing I can think of is a tornado."

The shopkeeper nodded. "Yup" he said, "at least we get some warning about the hurricanes. Funny how sales change when they're on the way though. Best time for us to sell batteries of course, and I know the lumber yards get lots of plywood sales but just about everything else slows down." He paused for a moment in thought, then added, "Had a peculiar sale this morning though."

Cameron asked, "Really? What was that?"

"Well, I guess you heard about that ship idled just off the inlet?" On seeing Cameron nod agreement, he continued, "Two of the boys from the ship come in this morning in a van from our municipal airport. They put down a wad of cash for some video equipment."

Cameron's curiosity was piqued, but to avoid looking too curious, he kept the conversation centered on the weather. "They must be getting bored out there," he said and continued, "I heard Mary's up to a category four. You'd think the crew would be pretty anxious, dead in the water like that. Hope they get the rudder going or they'll have to abandon ship I guess."

"Well you know the fellas that were in here said most of the crew were off the ship already but them two had to go back and wait 'til the last minute in case they get 'er going." His next comment was riveting. "Funniest thing though. I don't know what they're doing with such on a ship but they started asking me if I knew anything about fixing high tech tracking equipment."

Cameron could barely suppress his excitement when he asked, "Tracking equipment? Maybe they hunt in their off time?"

"Guess so. But sounds like awful fancy gear. Some kind of night goggles. They don't just have infrared, they got some kind of heat sensors so you can tell if an animal walked by within a certain amount of time."

"Boy, that is some fancy hunting," interjected Cameron. What kind of problem were they having with it?"

"Dunno. I told them I'd have to see it to tell. They just said they couldn't get it adjusted right and maybe they'd figure it out anyway."

Cameron asked laughingly, "You think they were foreigners? No telling how they hunt in some other countries."

"Didn't look or sound foreign to me. Best I could tell, they might have been Yankees. Guess that's kinda foreign." He let out a guffaw at his own joke and Cameron politely joined in.

Cameron said, "That's a whole different world up there anyway. Next thing you know, they'll have robots to do the hunting for them. Well, guess I better go. I still have to shutter the house. Take care."

"All right, you take care too. You know, we haven't had a hurricane hit category five since Hazel back in the '50s. I'd hate to think what could happen with all the building that's been going on here lately." Cameron just shook his head, gave a mock shudder, and left.

After he got back into his truck, Cameron again put on the communicator and within minutes heard Elliott's voice saying "Diamond Jim." When he answered the call, Elliott suggested another face-to-face meeting to relate new information. Cameron told Elliott he had news as well.

At the Gas Hog, Elliott pulled up to a gas pump behind Cameron and they both started gassing their vehicles. Cameron put the nozzle on automatic and sidled back to Elliott's car. Elliott said, "Your suggestion to try Virginia tags worked, sorta'. The car was a rental and the name and address given by the renter was phony. Here's the full tag number but I don't guess I should try to stop them until we can get a hold of Mr. Peterson."

"Speaking of," said Cameron, "I haven't heard from him all day."

"Me neither since this morning. Reckon he might have made it out to the ship?"

"I don't know. Let's hope we hear from him soon. I'm pretty well at a loss about what to do next. Anyway, I found out that somebody on board that ship has some high-tech tracking goggles that even have heat sensors. Man, I wish I knew what they were up to."

"Me too. Tracking goggles huh?" After musing for a moment, Elliott said, "Sounds like those two might have been what Mr. Peterson called 'Enforcers' or something. I wonder why they would need that kind of tracking equipment."

Cameron also took a moment to think, and spoke with an ever-so-slight quaver in his voice, saying, "Gene told us to be careful and we've seen what these boys will do. I hope we aren't the 'deer' they plan on hunting. Let's both be extra careful. Keep in touch. Oh, let's meet at the 'Java Hut' out near the airport next. It's open pretty late."

It was nearly seven when Cameron and Elliott went back out on the road. Cameron decided to drive to the Riverport waterfront. He wanted a few quiet moments before dark. He also wanted to see if he could manage to contact Peterson from a location near the water.

Fortunately, the small waterfront parking area was nearly empty. Cameron sat quietly, taking in the view and trying his best to relax for a while. After a few minutes his cell phone began buzzing. He didn't recognize the number on the caller ID but when he answered, it was Mary. She said, "Where in the world have you been? I've been trying to get up with you."

He replied, "Sorry, I've been all over town, and you know how spotty the cell service can be at times. You OK? Where are you?"

"Yes, I'm fine, still at work. What's going on?"

"Tell you what. Hang up and I'll call you right back. What phone are you using?"

"I'm on Callie's phone. Mine's been screwed up all day." Callie was another shift supervisor who was on vacation. She and Mary shared the same office but had different telephones.

"OK, talk to you in a minute." Cameron closed the cell phone, got out of his truck, and went across the street to a pay phone. He opened the cell phone again, recalled the last number received, and dialed it into the pay phone. Mary answered immediately saying, "What was that all about?"

Cameron responded, "Didn't want to use any of our usual phones. Don't know who's listening."

Mary said, "Ah, I understand. So what have you been doing?"

"Cruising and checking things out. Been finding out a few things but I still don't want to say much. I do need you to check on Sandy though. Larry took a ship up to Whittington this morning, and he's gone AWOL since then. I know she's got to be in panic mode."

"I'll get Lynn and Debbie to go over to her house. I'm sure she's frantic by now. I wish you'd told me sooner."

"I know, I know, but there's just been too much going on. I'm going to have Deputy Grainger go over there to talk to her. I'm just now grabbing a quick break on the waterfront. It's surprising how still the water is with a hurricane headed this way."

"I imagine things will pick up soon enough. I know it's been taking an odd path, but they're pretty sure we'll get at least part of it. Have you been able to do anything at the house?"

"'Fraid not. How about calling Monty's boy, Kenny, to get the loose stuff in the yard. We'll pay him double what we do for mowing. Now I'm glad we had those hurricane-glass storm windows put in."

"Me too. I'll try to get Kenny. Meantime, you be careful. I'm still watching a couple of people but I'm not even sure what I'm supposed to look for."

"Me either; just out-of-the-ordinary behavior is all I can say. Well, it's getting dark and I gotta go. Love you."

"Love you, too. Oh, with the storm coming, I'll probably be camped out here for a while, so don't look for me at home. Try to get inland as soon as you can. Bye, bye."

It had been good to hear Mary's voice, and after he hung up Cameron suddenly felt very much alone. He decided to get busy, first calling "Bee" and asking him to go by the Gullege house. He wanted Elliott to take the "official" missing person report to keep it out of regular channels, feeling that he, Peterson, or Elliott would probably find Larry faster than anyone at this point.

Cameron had one more lead he wanted to check out. Recalling that the electronics store owner told him the ship's crew members came to town in a shuttle van they rented at the local airport, Cameron wanted to see how they got from the ship to the airport.

On his drive to the airport Cameron kept an eye on the rearview mirror, hoping to see nothing unusual. His hopes were short-lived. As he turned onto the road leading to the airport, he saw a dark SUV make the turn several hundred feet behind him. When the car passed under a streetlight, he also noted that it had a front license plate; something required on Virginia cars but not North Carolina cars. The SUV stayed about a hundred yards behind, even as Cameron slowed to turn in to the airport entrance.

As he pulled into the parking lot Cameron lamented that he had not yet unlocked the glove compartment. Now he would have to turn the truck off to unlock it and retrieve the Glock he had borrowed from Sandy. While he pondered what to do, the SUV drove past the airport entrance and continued up the road until it was out of sight. Cameron felt foolish and paranoid.

The airport's fixed-base operator, Billy Howard, was in his office. Pulling a chair up to Billy's desk, Cameron said, "Ready for a canoing lesson?" Billy had taken several canoe lessons from Cameron already in preparation for a vacation trip to the mountains.

Billy answered, "At this time of night? You got to be crazy."

"Best time to see all the night critters is at night, you know."

"Uh huh. Tell you what, I'll take my next canoe lesson when you take your first flying lesson."

Cameron's usual response would have been, "No thanks, I feel safer on water", but for the night's purposes he said instead, "You know that's exactly why I'm here. Figured you wouldn't be as busy at night.

I've been reading a lot about that new sport flying certification and I wanted your take on it."

Billy answered, "Well it takes a lot less time to go solo, for one. Some veteran fliers think it's OK and some don't. I'm kind of in between. I got some brochures here somewhere that explain it better than I can. Why don't you take them home and look them over?"

"Thanks, I will. Course, I still prefer good old water transportation, but I might give it a try. You still keeping up the canoe practice? Not much time until your trip is it?"

"A few months yet. I've been meaning to call you. I sure as hell can't go out tonight though."

"That's all right, I was just kidding anyway." Cameron continued to steer the conversation, "Ever think about vacationing on a big boat?"

"You mean a motorboat?"

"No, one of the big cruise ships."

Billy pondered a moment. "Not really," he said, "Way too many people."

"Yeah, I guess you're right. To me, about the only thing big ships are good for is getting lots of cargo someplace."

Billy countered, "I'm not even so sure about that. I guess you've heard there's a cargo freighter stalled near the inlet?"

Cameron feigned ignorance. "I heard something about it. Didn't one of their engines break down or something?"

"Not an engine really. It was the rudder motor. Had some of the crew in here the other day and they were telling me about it. The motor burned out right when they reached the shoals and they nearly grounded."

"Some of the crew? What were they doing here?"

Billy responded, "They needed some ground transportation and rented one of our vans." To Cameron's unasked question, he answered. "It's not unusual for some of those freighters to have a two or four man helicopter on board for various reasons. They flew it in here after they found out we rent vehicles."

Cameron said, "Well you learn something new every day." In fact, Cameron had learned much more than Billy could imagine. He continued, "Well if you don't want to get your 'night wings'- or should I say 'night paddles'- I guess I'll mosey along. Tell Veronica I said hello. Oh, and I'll be sure to read these brochures and get in touch."

"OK, you tell Mary hello for me. You ready for the storm?"

"Just about. Got a few little things to do, then it's mostly waiting. See you." On his way to the truck Cameron paused a moment to admire the full moon that now brightened the night sky.

As soon as Cameron entered his truck he unlocked the glove compartment and transferred the Glock to his waistband. Then he checked in with Elliott on the communicator, telling him they needed to meet again. When they met at the Java Hut, Cameron told Elliott how the ship's crew got to the airport.

Elliott responded, "Helicopter huh? This thing gets weirder and weirder. Still haven't heard from Mr. Peterson, but I got to see Sandy Gullege. She's worried sick now and I can't say as I blame her. I told her we'd do everything we could."

"OK, thanks Elliott. Was there anybody there when you left?"

"Yeah, a couple of friends of hers said they'd stay right with her."

"Good. I guess we better get on the road again. Hey, is that transponder on my truck still working?"

"Yup. I haven't been tracking you lately. Don't really need to now. But it's good for about a month."

"Good. How about keeping tabs on me, it'll make me feel a little safer. Let's make the parking lot at 'Harvey's Grocery' our next meet place."

"Ten-four. Talk to you later."

As Elliott drove away, Cameron sat in his car and pondered. Neither of them had a clue where all the developments were leading but Cameron had a strong hunch Larry's disappearance was connected to the 'High Sea Soprano' and its crew. He also had a strong hunch that the ship was central to whatever the organization planned to do.

A sudden urge to get to the ship and find out something, anything, welled up within Cameron. Images of helicopters, ships, Level Twos, Fours, category five, shadowy figures, all started swirling and blending into each other. Cameron forced himself to sit back and take several deep breaths to shake the panic. After several minutes he still felt shaky but settled enough to be on his way, wherever that may be. He locked the communicator in the glove box and drove away.

CHAPTER TWENTY-SIX

Cameron saw no traffic either direction as he turned from the Java Hut on to the main road. Shortly however, he spotted a vehicle falling in behind him with its lights off. He could make out the shape of it under the full moon and was fairly certain that it was the same SUV that followed him earlier.

The car stayed about a hundred yards behind, as it had before Cameron drove into the airport. If he sped up it sped up, if he slowed it slowed, as if tethered to his car by a long rod.

Nearing the road to Riverport, Cameron switched on his right turn signal as if going back to town. Seeing no oncoming traffic he made a sudden left turn instead, flooring the gas pedal as the truck straightened. The SUV turned behind him and began catching up. He made another sudden left onto a dirt road, almost losing control as the truck fishtailed in the loose sand. Cameron floored it again and cut off his headlights. In the mirror he could see bright moonlight glinting off the SUV's chrome bumper as it careened around the turn. Again it quickly gained on him. About this time Cameron realized that he was instinctively making his way back to the cabin and its familiar woods.

As Cameron made a hard right onto another dirt road he thought, "*Damn, my dust trail's way too easy to follow. Then again, they may not know how far ahead I am.*" The thought was dispelled in a heartbeat. His teeth rattled as the pursuing SUV slammed into the back of his truck, nearly spinning it out of control again. The truck skidded to the right up a shallow embankment, throwing rocks and grass every direction. Overcompensating to get back on the road, Cameron steered hard to the left. The truck fishtailed to the other side and sideswiped a higher embankment that steered it back to the middle of the road.

When he finally regained control of his truck, Cameron looked in the mirror once again but could see nothing through the haze of dust behind him. He thought, *"s.o.b.s must not have realized they were so close coming through the dust. I hope to hell they wrecked. I ain't gonna' stay to find out though"*, as he sped through the night to the cabin.

For a fleeting moment Cameron thought of the transponder attached to his truck. *"Funny, here I was telling Elliott I was glad I had it"* he recalled. *"Now I don't know if I'm advertising my whereabouts to every nut out there. Hell, no time to take it off now."* Cameron wrestled the cell phone from his pocket only to be frustrated when it read "No Signal". Cursing, he stuffed it back into his pocket. In the excitement, use of the communicator did not even cross his mind.

When he reached the cabin entry drive, Cameron decided it was too overgrown to risk driving through it in the dark. Instead he purposely spun the truck into its usual parking place across the road. He knew that position would give him a better view of any oncoming vehicles as well.

After the dust settled, Cameron could see a roostertail of dust about a quarter mile up the road, moving rapidly toward him. Pulling the Glock pistol from his waistband as he jumped out of the truck, he tore straight across the road and up the cabin path. Just then he remembered the communicator and smacked himself across the forehead for leaving it behind. As he raced down the path, he heard the SUV roaring to a stop and its doors slamming.

CHAPTER TWENTY-SEVEN

The green Explorer with Virginia tags and four occupants skidded to a stop a few feet from Cameron's front bumper. While the driver and front seat passenger remained in the car, two men jumped out of the back seat. One was tall and heavyset with a short sloping forehead; the other was short and wiry, with a pinched face. They hurriedly put on bulky goggles and adjusted some switches and dials. Then, pistols drawn, they rushed to the wooded path, focusing on the traces of Cameron's footsteps that were illuminated by the high-tech eyewear.

The path narrowed as the men barreled on, ever thickening shrubs hemming them in on the sides and branches slapping them from above. Still they pursued, heads down like two hounds, focused on the footprints. At the thickest overgrowth just before the swamp they stopped, momentarily perplexed. The footsteps had disappeared. They looked at the ground all around, and played with the dials on their goggles. The heavy one spoke: "I told you these damn things weren't right; mine just quit working."

The wiry one impatiently retorted, "The ground's wetter here so it probably cools off the prints faster. Just take 'em off and keep going." He tore off the goggles and plunged headlong through the thicket into the swampy, open part of the path. The heavy man ripped off his goggles and followed a few feet behind.

Too late, the men discovered that they should have worn the goggles for infrared night vision. The skinny one tripped over a large, solid object in the path and suddenly felt a tremendous searing pain in his right leg. Hearing screams of terror, the heavy man squinted into the darkness. In the dim moonlight, he could barely see the alligator

113

dragging his companion toward the swamp. He tried to take aim on the moving target.

In pain and desperation, the wiry man began shooting wildly toward the thing that had him in its grip. He did not hear his partner hit the ground when one of those wild shots tore through the heavy man's sloped forehead. In fact, all he could hear by then was the rush of cool black swamp water past his ears.

Then, all was quiet. The usual chirps, buzzes, hums and assorted sounds of a summer night had ceased for the moment. From his perch in the branches above the path, all Cameron could hear was his heart pounding and blood rushing through his veins. He was too stunned to move. As he hoped, his pursuers were so intent on looking down for his footprints they did not think to look overhead. He had planned to backtrack to the road as they continued toward the cabin, but did not expect Mother Nature to intervene on his behalf.

Still shaking, Cameron extricated himself from the tangle of branches that had held him aloft, and gingerly climbed back down to the path. For several minutes he stood motionless, listening for footsteps and trying to calm his nerves. Although his heart had slowed somewhat, he still found it difficult to hear over the rushing in his ears. Finally satisfied that no one else was coming down the path, he retraced his route to the road, pistol in hand. Soon he reached a point in the trail where he could see his Ram and the SUV across the road. Sidestepping off the trail and into the brush, he peered through the leaves.

The Explorer's headlights were on now, illuminating Cameron's truck. The Ram's hood was raised and one man was leaning into the engine compartment. In the reflected light, Cameron could see another man sitting behind the wheel of the Explorer. Fearing that they were trying to disable his pickup and trap him, Cameron quickly devised a plan. He fished in his left pocket for his keyring, hoping to catch them off guard by remotely starting the truck. He also hoped it would startle them enough to give him the advantage if it came to a shootout. Aiming the Glock with his right hand, he pushed the start button with his left.

Fortunately the undergrowth absorbed much of the concussion, but Cameron was still thrown back several feet as the explosives being planted in his truck detonated. The blast tore the front ends off both vehicles and the ensuing inferno incinerated the remaining two

Enforcers. Even from the shelter of the woods, Cameron could feel the intense heat.

As he recovered and tried to regain his footing, Cameron had the incongruous thought that this was going to be awfully hard to explain to the insurance adjuster.

CHAPTER TWENTY-EIGHT

Once he got back on his feet, Cameron peered across the road. The gruesome sight made him momentarily nauseous and he quickly averted his gaze. He thought, *"How in the hell did I get myself into this? And how am I going to get myself out of it?"* Peeking across the road one more time, he tried to see the back of his truck. He hoped the tag was obliterated, saying out loud, "Please don't let anybody find out that was my truck." The sound of his own voice echoing through the woods startled him, and he silently pleaded, "And please don't anybody call Mary to tell her what they found."

Cameron had a sinking feeling as he pondered his next move , and thought, *"Oh shit, the communicator got incinerated with my truck."* When he pulled the cell phone from his right pocket hoping to contact Elliott, he realized how lucky he had been so far. One of the wild shots fired by the wiry man had grazed his pocket and shattered the phone's earpiece on the way through. In the noise and confusion, he hadn't even felt it. Now, he had no transportation and no means of communication.

With no other direction to go, Cameron headed toward the cabin, peering very carefully down the swamp path before traversing it. Once inside the cabin, he started to turn on the power but thought better of it. Instead he sat in the dark for a while, trying to calm himself and think of a course of action.

Thought after thought tumbled through Cameron's mind. *"All right, this is a battle and I've got to steel my nerves for battle. They blew themselves up, they're gone, and that's that. It could've been me. It was supposed to be me."* After an involuntary shudder, he continued his thoughts, *"All right, don't dwell on it, think about the future. What the hell are you going to do now? Damn, I'm hungry."*

Realizing it had been quite a while since he'd had anything to eat, Cameron hunted through the meager supplies left in the kitchen and assembled a meal of peanut butter, stale saltines and bottled water. Next, he ambled out to the front porch to eat, think, and listen for anyone approaching. As he munched his first cracker he surveyed the waterway and the ocean, wishing Mary was by his side to see the moonlight reflecting off the tranquil waters. He allowed the serenity of the scene to soothe him, clearing his mind so he could figure out what to do next. His gaze wandered aimlessly over countless constellations in the sky to iridescent points of light in the distant ocean.

Cameron stopped scanning the horizon when his eyes focused on some brighter lights. It dawned on him that it was The High Sea Soprano, still idling where he had seen it before. It also struck him that the Soprano was the only vessel he could detect on the water. Then he recalled, "I guess Hurricane Mary's still out there somewhere barreling toward us. I bet everyone else has got their boats secured. So why hasn't the Soprano even gotten towed into port yet?"

As he watched the distant lights, Cameron's attention was drawn to the sound of equally distant sirens. He got up and walked to one end of the porch, where he could see a faint glow from the burning vehicles. In his earlier daze he had not contemplated that the fire might ignite the adjacent field or woods, but it did not appear to be spreading. He thought, "I don't know how long it's going to take for them to find out where the fire is, so I'd better get busy."

Cameron started piecing together some of the clues he already knew. *"All right, the goons who were chasing me had to be from that ship"* he reasoned. *"They were some of the crew who asked about getting the goggles fixed at the electronics store. Lucky for me they didn't get that worked out. Larry's missing and Larry's a river pilot. Somebody needs him to guide them up river. Why? I don't know, but the Soprano's got to to be key to whatever they're about to do.*

"Seas are going to pick up real soon with Hurricane Mary getting closer. I can't believe it's still so calm out there. They've got to know the hurricane's coming, so surely they're going to make their move soon. I can't get hold of Elliott or Peterson. For all I know, Peterson's on the Soprano and something's happened to him. I don't know what else to do; I've got to get on that ship."

117

Presently, a faint buzz caught Cameron's ear. He immediately thought of his hornet nightmare of what now seemed eons ago. Turning toward the source of the sound, and seeing a small light moving along the waterway, he realized that it was a night fisherman using an older, noisier battery-operated trolling motor. *"Well,"* he thought, *"guess he figured he'd catch a few more while he still could."*

Then it struck him; of course; that was it. His canoe was racked behind the cabin, and on the cabin floor were his trolling motor and fully-charged batteries. If the seas remained calm as they were, he might just have a chance to make it. He rushed inside to gather the motor and batteries.

As he lugged the motor down the hill to the pier, Cameron reminisced about the many fishing excursions he and Mary had taken in the canoe. The trolling motor helped them reach distant locations faster and he even made some outriggers to clamp on it for stability while motoring. With the outriggers in place, the size and shape of the canoe allowed speeds up to fourteen knots in good conditions.

When he went back for the batteries, Cameron estimated how far out the Soprano was, then he looked at a tide clock he kept in the living room. Good news; ebb tide was just starting and it would give him a strong outgoing current. If all went well, he could reach the ship within two hours. Even though his newer motor was much quieter than the one he just heard on the creek, he felt it best to paddle the last quarter mile or so. He hoped the ship would still be at anchor when he reached it. He also hoped that he would have enough energy to scale the anchor chain and get aboard, since he was not familiar with any other way to board a ship uninvited. He thought he remembered reading somewhere that modern-day pirates often used the anchor chain to board ships.

After throwing together a few more cracker and peanut butter sandwiches, Cameron grabbed a full bottle of water, made a quick pit-stop in the bathroom, and hurried to the canoe rack at the back of the cabin. The sirens were growing louder now and he figured the firefighters must have gotten their bearings. He did not want to be around when they arrived.

Cameron strapped the paddles to the canoe's thwarts, attached the outriggers and put on his life vest. He didn't have time for a regular carry, and just dragged the canoe down the hill. Soon he had the motor attached amidships and was underway. By the time he entered the Waterway, he estimated by the sound of the sirens that the fire trucks had finally reached their destination.

As he steered the boat out of the river and into the waterway, Cameron took a look back at the cabin, hoping it was not the last time he set eyes on it.

CHAPTER TWENTY-NINE

The last emergency vehicle reaching the twisted, smoldering ruins was a deputy's cruiser. As the firefighters hosed down the remaining flames, Elliott stepped out of his car and walked to the back of what appeared to have been a pickup truck. His powerful flashlight cut through the dust and smoke to the rear bumper, but the license was too far gone for him to make out the letters or numbers. He could, however, make out the indented letters in the tailgate that spelled "Dodge".

Elliott returned to the cruiser. He donned the communicator and once more spoke the words "Diamond Jim", as he had been doing numerous times over the last hour. Earlier he got a broken response when calling for "Butterfly" but was unable to maintain contact long enough to hear anything intelligible. Now he was afraid he waited too long to track Cameron. By the time he had turned on his computer, the transponder's image only blinked for a few seconds then disappeared. Elliott feared the worst but tried to remain optimistic.

Leaving the communicator in the car, Elliott returned to the smoking wreckage. The flames were out and the metal was cooling, so he could get closer to inspect the carnage. After gingerly stepping through mud and over hoses and other firefighting apparatus, he shined the flashlight beam into what was left of the truck's cab, relieved to find no apparent sign of an occupant.

Stepping to the driver's side of the SUV, he shined the light inside and viewed the charred remains of a human form. Then he shined the light in a wider arc around the vehicles and saw a human arm about seventy-five feet away in a field. Although the arm was somewhat charred, it was still covered with most of the sleeve of a denim shirt. Walking over to take a closer look he could see that it was a left arm, the hand still clutched tightly around a set of pliers.

Elliott returned to the vehicles and discerned more charred body parts scattered around the fronts of both. As he called for detectives on his walkie-talkie, a hint of relief crossed his face. He recalled that none of the fingers on the hand clutching the pliers had a ring on it. He remembered observing a wedding ring on Cameron's left hand; one that had been worn so long that it would not be easily dislodged.

After he got off the walkie-talkie, Elliott played his flashlight on the road in the immediate area around the wreckage. Within several feet of the vehicles there was only mud and the bootprints of firefighters, but several sets of footprints appeared on the wooded side of the road leading toward a pathway. He read nothing into the prints, choosing simply to see where they led, but thought it odd that only one set of prints seemed to go both directions. Shortly he found a body on the path and another, badly mangled, floating face-up in the swamp not too far away. He again called the detectives to relate his find, and again felt relieved that he did not recognize either corpse.

Only one set of footprints continued from that point and Elliott followed them to the cabin, where they disappeared in the drier ground. The doors were locked and the windows shuttered but fresh cracker crumbs littered the front porch. Elliott observed freshly trampled grass and drag marks leading down the hill and followed those traces. As he walked out on the the pier, he saw more cracker crumbs. Recalling an earlier invitation from Cameron to come to the cabin for canoe-fishing, Elliott smiled, shook his head, and said aloud, "That dumb-ass is gonna try to paddle his way out to the Soprano. Hope to hell he makes it."

By the time Elliott found his way back to the road, the detectives were just arriving. He told them where to find the other bodies, reporting falsely that he had checked further down the path and found nothing. As a red herring he told the detectives that it looked like a drug deal gone bad, hoping it would buy Cameron time to accomplish whatever he was trying to do.

Looking at his watch, Elliott realized that it was past the end of his shift. He figured the best thing he could do now was to go home and get some rest until someone could resume contact.

CHAPTER THIRTY

With a full moon lighting the way and a strong ebb tide pushing the canoe, Cameron made his way to open sea in good time. After a while on open water he thought, "This is as bad as driving the Interstate, except there's no billboards for entertainment." He could see the Soprano's lights but the perspective never seemed to change; the lights seemed as far away after an hour as they had when he started. "Guess I ought to enjoy the salt air and cool breeze while I can" he mused, "No telling when it'll be this quiet again."

Bit by bit, the shape of the Soprano became more discernible, appearing to grow larger as Cameron drew closer. He noticed that the oncoming swells were increasing in frequency and intensity; not enough to capsize his canoe but enough to slow him down a bit. Wispy clouds began dancing across the sky as well; scouts for the advancing horde of flash and fury.

At a place that he estimated to be a quarter mile or so from the ship, Cameron unlashed one of the broad paddles from the thwarts before stilling the trolling motor and raising it from the water. The outriggers could wait until he was much closer; the noise of raising them would not be amplified in his composite-plastic canoe as it would in an aluminum canoe. He immediately began paddling toward the Soprano.

The ship loomed ever larger as Cameron drew closer. When he was within a hundred yards of it he unclamped the outriggers, thinking, "*All right time for you to go, you'll just be in the way,*" and pushed them away. During the process the canoe turned somewhat obliquely into a swell, tipped sideways, and came precariously close to swamping. Cameron scrambled to get the canoe stabilized, paddling furiously to get back on track.

The last hundred yards was the hardest as Cameron paddled against the rising sea and increasing winds. It seemed to him that for each foot he moved forward, he was pushed back two. He squinted against the intermittent sprays of salt water that slapped across his face, stinging his eyes.

Finally Cameron was at the bow of the ship, its bulk blotting out what moonlight was not covered by increasing clouds. As he paddled toward the anchor chain he mused, *"At least I've got a little shelter from the wind here."* But as he looked up, he could not even see the top of the huge black hulk hovering over him. He worried, *"What was I thinking? I'll never get up there. What the hell, I'll never get back home either. Doesn't look like there's much place to go but up."*

Cameron unclasped and removed the life jacket to allow himself more flexibility, and let it drop into the canoe. Maneuvering his craft as deftly as he could toward the anchor chain, he tried to get a feeling for the rise and fall of the swells, knowing there would be little room for error. Already his shoulders were aching from the exertion.

After making some swift calculations, Cameron positioned the canoe to the rear of the chain, heading toward the ship's stern and facing an oncoming swell. As it rose, he paddled furiously down from its crest into its trough. Then he extended a hard sweep of the paddle and did an about-face, now heading the same direction as the ship. As the next swell carried him upward he again paddled hard, steering the canoe's bow just past the anchor chain. As the canoe reached the apex of the swell, its midsection came to the chain, where Cameron grabbed the nearest link and hoisted himself up and out. He gained a foothold just in time to watch his canoe disappear into the darkness.

Cameron quickly climbed several links to avoid the rising swells, then stopped and hung on to rest before continuing upward. The large chain used on the Soprano had a crossbar on each link, giving Cameron a good handhold. However, getting a good foothold proved much more difficult; he could barely fit the toe of his shoe into the crossbars. He knew he had to use the crossbars; movement of the chain where the links were joined could crush his hands or feet.

Straining to gain every inch on his way up the chain, Cameron finally reached the hawespipe, the opening for passage of the chain into the ship. Fortunately the hawespipe was on the main deck and it gave him the footing to hoist himself over the rail. His soft-soled shoes made little noise as he landed on deck. So exhausted that he could barely move, he hoped no one could see or hear him as he laid down in the shadows gasping for breath. Although his breath was still labored, after a few minutes he could sit up with his back against the bulwarks and survey the scene before him.

From his vantage point Cameron could see the ship's tall superstructure at the stern, looking like a five-story building perched atop the deck. Near the top of the superstructure was the bridge and in its low lighting he could discern some movement. A low rumble, one he felt more than heard, told him that the ship's engines were idling. As he sat, his breath getting back to normal, he thought, *"All right, getting up here was one miracle. Wonder how many I have left?"*

After regaining his wind, Cameron stealthily began working his way aft to the superstructure. Suddenly hearing voices coming toward him, he ducked into a dark alcove between some shipping containers that were lashed to the deck. From the shadows, he could see two crewmen walking toward the bow. They stopped nearby as if waiting for something and began talking to each other. Cameron barely breathed as he listened. "I can't believe we gotta take the chopper back out with a hurricane coming," said the first. "Why the hell do we gotta go to the nuke plant?" The other responded, "We're just supposed to set off some perimeter alarms and get the hell out is all I know. Somebody else is goin' in. Hell, nobody tells us nothin'. I still don't know why we had to take them special goggles to the other guys yesterday."

Before the first man could respond, a bank of lights came on, illuminating the bow deck, and they hurried to their stations. Cameron gingerly peeked out from behind the container and watched them take positions near the capstan and anchor chain on the forward deck. One of them spoke into a walkie-talkie and instantly the air was filled with the din of moving machinery and chains. Seeing that the men's attention was focused on the incoming anchor chain, Cameron moved on. He thought, *"Larry's got to be on the bridge if they're getting ready to move. I've got to get up there. Looks like they got the rudder motor fixed, if it was ever been broken in the first place."*

The few shipping containers stacked on deck provided cover as Cameron furtively made his way to the stern. To his surprise he encountered no other crew members on deck but took it as a momentary blessing; he could move quickly toward the superstructure undetected. Noting that no helicopter was in sight, he thought there might be a landing platform somewhere behind the bridge.

Cameron finally reached the superstructure and looked up at the massive flat front, pierced here and there by portholes. About four stories up, he could see what looked like several long picture windows glowing orange in the night sky; the bridge. From his angle far below, he could not see inside. From where he stood, hiding behind a container on the left, or port side of the ship, he could make out an open breezeway flanking the side of the superstructure on the first level.

Easing his way down the breezeway, Cameron found a steel door in a dimly lit section of the wall and eased it open, peering cautiously inside. In front of him was a hallway that appeared to stretch to the far side of the ship, with doors on either side. Although no one was in sight, he could hear muffled voices not far away. He stepped through the door and gently pulled it almost shut and then crept as noiselessly as he could toward the sound of the voices.

Cameron could hear two voices, one male and one female, emanating loudly from behind one of the doors. The female voice was low-toned. After working with many transplanted Northerners in his practice, Cameron thought he recognized a South Jersey twang in her speech.

"Look, I don't see any other choice," she said.

The male responded, "I don't like it. I think we need to head away from the storm and wait for another time." Cameron thought he detected something vaguely familiar in the man's voice.

The female replied, "There's too damn much in place for us to quit now. We already lost too much time when that idiot messenger got caught. Besides, we've got nothing but a skeleton crew left here."

The man said, "Well, it would be nice to know what our mission is. I think the Level Fours keep too much to themselves. I understand they want security, but I think they put the whole project in danger by compartmentalizing too much."

The female's voice took on a threatening tone. "You're lucky I'm the only one to hear you talk like that. The captain knows what's going to happen, and you'll know soon enough. Go on to the bridge. I'll get the river pilot and meet you there."

Cameron quickly turned and rushed tip-toe to the entry door. He barely had time to step out and ease it mostly shut as he heard the hallway door open. As he hurried down the breezeway looking for a hiding place, he had a gut-wrenching realization; the man he just heard was Gene Peterson.

CHAPTER THIRTY-ONE

Cameron found a shadowy niche between some containers and tried to squeeze into a tight ball, wishing he could just disappear. He cupped his face in his hands, taking deep breaths, trying to organize his thoughts. He could feel the throb of the engines, and knew that they now were underway. Where were they headed? Apparently not out to sea and into the hurricane. And how could he have let himself be taken in by Peterson? Why had Peterson drawn him this far into the whole scheme? He felt very much alone, betrayed, and frightened.

Cameron heard increasing winds whistle ominously through the Soprano's various cables and wires and he could feel the ship begin to pitch and roll on the growing waves. He thought, *"OK Mary, I don't know where you've been hiding 'til now, but please go easy on us now that you're here."* He could only pray the hurricane would not surpass category two or three.

Just as Cameron regained his composure enough to start thinking of a plan, he felt something cold and hard against his temple and froze. The words that followed were spoken in a gruff whisper, but pierced through him as though they had been screamed in his ear. "Hands where I can see them, and come out crawling," ordered Peterson from behind him. As Cameron unraveled and crawled backwards into the open, the barrel of the pistol never left his temple. Once they were fully in the open, Peterson said, "All right, now slowly turn where I can see you."

Cameron slowly turned and gazed up at Peterson, who was wearing the same type of goggles Cameron had seen on his pursuers earlier in the evening, or the evening before; he was no longer sure what time of day it was. Peterson stood frozen for a moment, still aiming the pistol, and Cameron braced himself for the concussion to follow. But no shot was fired. Instead, Peterson ripped the goggles from his head, lowered the pistol, and stood staring blankly for a few seconds more.

Finally Peterson broke the silence, still whispering, "Holy crap, you're alive!"

"Yeah, I'm afraid your buddies didn't get me. You'll have to finish the job for them, I suppose."

Peterson's only response, still whispered, was, "Holy crap."

Cameron hissed back, "Will you stop saying that. Look, if you're going to shoot me, go on and get it over with." At the same time, he slowly slid his right hand toward his waistband.

Peterson reacted quickly, instinctively raising his pistol again and slapping Cameron's hand away from the Glock. He then clamped a hand around Cameron's elbow and all but dragged him back to the breezeway and into the hall Cameron had left minutes before. He motioned Cameron to walk down the hall in front of him, then rapped on his shoulder when they reached the room where Cameron had heard the voices. Opening the door, he pushed Cameron into the room, then pulled the door shut and locked it.

Finally Peterson spoke, still in subdued tones. "I don't know how you got away from those goons, much less how the hell you found your way onto this ship," he said, "but I'm sure as hell glad to see you."

"You've got some way of showing it," retorted Cameron. "This is the second time you've nearly made me crap myself with that gun. Next time you point it at me, just go on and shoot. Why are you even keeping me alive now? Aren't I screwing up whatever you and your friends have planned? And how the hell did you know I was here in the first place?"

"Cameron, just shut up a minute and listen. I haven't got that much time to explain but first, these people aren't my friends now any more than they've ever been. I really couldn't tell even you and Elliott that they think I'm one of them. I still don't know exactly what's about to happen, but I think you heard me trying to find out. I do know this ship is loaded with enough explosives to level Riverport, most of them in the containers on the top deck."

Cameron could do nothing for the moment but blink in astonishment, so Peterson continued, "Speaking of Elliott, have you heard anything from him? I made brief contact once, but the signal was too broken."

"I haven't heard anything since sometime before my little encounter with your buddies. Elliott did mention your attempt to reach him, though. He probably doesn't know if we're alive or dead. How much did you know about what they were trying to do to me?"

"I know they were afraid you found out too much. I told them I had you convinced I was working on a drug sting and that you were pretty much out of it, but I was overruled. When I could steal a minute I tried to reach you and got nothing, and then I had that failed contact with Elliott. We heard the explosion and saw the flames even from out here, so everybody assumed they'd finished you off. Cameron, you've got to believe me, I couldn't do more to warn you without jeopardizing the whole investigation, and you see how vital it is for me to keep up the double identity."

Cameron only stared back coldly in response.

"As for how I found you just now," continued Peterson, "I was the first one out of this room a while ago. Out of the corner of my eye, I caught a glimpse of the hallway door swinging shut before my 'companion' came out. I knew where everybody else should be, so I figured somebody new must have gotten on board. I let her go to the bridge and grabbed the extra night-vision goggles, hoping I could find out who it was. I get the feeling you've seen some like them already today."

Cameron nodded but still said nothing.

"Anyway, I had no idea it was you until you turned around," continued Peterson. "If we live through all this, you're going to have to tell me what happened back there, and especially how the hell you got on this ship, but we don't have time now. I've got to get up to the bridge before they wonder what I'm doing. I think you'll be safe in here, it's my cabin."

Cameron was still leery, but he asked, "How will I know what's going on?"

"I'll try to find a way to let you know. In the meantime, keep your pistol ready. If anybody comes in this room unannounced, shoot first and don't worry about asking questions. If it's me, I'll scratch on the door three times first. By the way, if you still don't trust me keep in mind that I haven't taken away your firearm. All right, gotta go. Just keep your guard up." He started to open the door.

129

Cameron stopped him by saying, "In case you're interested, they're all dead."

"Who?"

"The goons who were chasing me. They kind of did themselves in."

Peterson countered with a wry smile. Then he slowly opened the door and peered down the hall both ways before slipping out. Once he was alone, Cameron looked around the room. It appeared to be a small combination office and stateroom with a small bathroom to one side. He promptly made use of the facility, after which he settled into a chair to wait. For how long, he had no idea.

CHAPTER THIRTY-TWO

After leaving Cameron behind, Peterson climbed the stairs to the bridge, explained to those who were waiting that he had to make a 'pit stop' on the way, and then stood waiting. In the orange glow of the bridge's nighttime lighting he could see the Captain, the woman with the South Jersey accent, and Larry, whose hands were cuffed behind his back. The only other people he knew to be aboard at this point were Cameron and the two crew members who secured the anchor earlier.

Peterson said, "Anybody want to let me in on what we're doing now? We don't seem to have much crew left."

The woman glared at Peterson, but the Captain said, "Fair enough. It's time for you to know. Let me tell you what's happened and then I'll tell you what's going to happen.

"Most of the crew that I sent ashore earlier in the week don't have a clue what we're doing. You know that I sent Waters, Vanucci and Drew ashore yesterday to go after Lawyer Scott. They met up with Harrison, our guy that's been living there, to do the job. I'm pretty sure they got him. Some deputy on the scene, Grainger I think his name was, reported that the lawyer and his truck got blown up. Problem is, we lost all four of our enforcers in the process."

Larry blurted out, "You son of a bitch, that lawyer was one of my buddies."

The woman moved to backhand Larry but the Captain said, "Leave him alone. We need him to be alert." Speaking to Larry he said, "There's too many lawyers around anyway. We're going to fix that when we take over. Meantime, keep your mouth shut unless you're giving directions."

Continuing his narrative to Peterson, the Captain said, "The helicopter pilot and a few other crew members that had to stay aboard weren't part of our group but they learned a little more than they should." Pointing to the female, he said, "Tanya here sent them overboard early this morning. You might have heard the splashes. I don't think they'll surface for quite a while."

Tanya and the Captain laughed as if they had just heard a great joke. Larry grumbled to himself, prompting The Captain to tell him, "My boy, this is war. I know you served some time in the military, so you understand the need for certain... tactics. Now you just keep giving us the calls and Tanya might let you go when we're all done. Otherwise, she'll drop you right here and we'll take our chances with the river. Understand?" Tanya pulled a forty-five automatic pistol from a holster and jammed it into Larry's ribs.

Larry said bitterly, "Yeah I understand." He continued calling out turns so the Captain could steer the ship past shallows and dangerous shoals on the way to the river inlet.

Peterson asked the Captain, "Mind telling me your story? I mean, what got you into the group?"

The Captain replied, "Curious peckerhead, aren't you? What the hell, doesn't make a difference now anyway. I was a Coast Guard Frigate Captain until some dumbass yacht jockey cut too close in front of my ship. Some rich politician's son was aboard, so I had to take the blame for sinking it. They busted me down to a desk job. Freakin' politicians. Speaking to Peterson, he asked, "What about you, Jensen? What'd the FBI do to you?"

"Me? Sort of the same, but without the ship. Made a huge drug bust that should have got me promoted, but some politician's daughter got caught up in it. Didn't get busted but they stuck me behind a desk too. All that damn work, a good clean bust and... pfft. Know what I mean?"

The Captain repeated, "Freakin' politicians." He pointed a thumb toward Tanya and said, "Get a load of her story. Tell him, Tanya."

Her only reply was, "I don't want to talk about it."

"Fine, I'll tell him," said the Captain.

"Look," she replied, pointing at Peterson, "I really don't even know this guy. I hardly even know you. So why don't we just do our jobs and quit running our mouths, OK?"

132

"She worked for the State Department and a politician's daughter got the promotion she should have," the Captain said with a sidelong glance at Peterson.

"Damn it, I said shut up," shouted Tanya, turning her pistol toward the Captain.

In one swift motion the Captain pulled a revolver from his waistband, cocked it, and pointed it directly at Tanya's temple, saying in a calm, measured voice, "If we didn't need your brains for the next phase they'd be splattered on the far side of this bridge. Now point that thing where you're supposed to and we'll pretend nothing happened."

For a few seconds the two stood in a standoff, glaring at each other. Tanya then took a deep breath and said, "Sorry, I'm trying to concentrate on getting our mission done. I'm just not in the mood for small talk."

The Captain responded, "Understood. We'll concentrate on the mission. But you keep in mind that I'm the only Level Four on this ship and you answer to me."

She replied with a surly "Yes sir."

He added, "One more thing; I don't care whether you know Jensen or not. He's here to pilot the chopper for me and he's not part of your crew."

They all spent the next ten minutes in a silence broken only by Larry's occasional command to turn the ship a particular direction. After a while the captain spoke, keeping his eye on the waters ahead. "All right, here's what's going to happen. When we get further upriver, where we're going to 'lose' our steering again. I'll alert the authorities, but they won't do anything after I tell them we're grounded away from the main channel and can get ourselves ashore. They'll have enough to handle on land once the storm gets here."

The Captain steered through a few tight turns and continued, "Pegram and Roznik are on the main deck now. They started arming the charges in the containers once they got the anchor secured. When they're done they'll come up here." He pointed to Tanya and continued, "You'll go with them and launch the portside bridge lifeboat when we get past Riverport, and go to the western bank. A car will be waiting and you know where to go from there."

The Captain next said to Peterson, "Jensen, I want you to go below and ready the chopper. Keep it secured, but once we reach our destination we'll drop the aft ramp and you'll fly us out through the opening. It's too rough now to bring it topside with the crane. If we're lucky, the wind won't be as bad upriver."

Peterson asked, "Are you sure we're going to have enough time before the charges go off?"

"We'll have plenty of time. The storm will help, because we can drop anchor mid-channel and nobody'll be on the river to know the difference. The charges will go off at 6:00 a.m.. That's the signal for phase two to start in earnest. Tanya, you, Pegram and Roznik will give the heads-up to our phase two operatives on shore."

Tanya asked, "What's the point of blowing this boat up, and what's phase two going to be?"

Acerbically, the Captain pointed out to Tanya, "It's a ship, not a boat, and the point of blowing it up is to block the shipping channel for now. Phase two is none of our concern. Our job is to complete our immediate mission, as you've pointed out."

Scattered throughout the whole conversation was Larry's intermittent calling of courses for the Captain to steer, which prompted Peterson to point to Larry and ask, "What about him?"

The captain replied, "He'll go off with us." Tanya shot a glance at Peterson that told him Larry would never leave the ship. Then the Captain barked at Peterson, "Didn't I give you a task to do? Get it done, then report back here. When Tanya leaves, you'll have to keep watch on pilot-boy here."

Peterson hurried down to the room where he had left Cameron, barely remembering to scratch on the door first. Cameron had the Glock in hand as he cautiously eased the door open. Peterson locked the door behind him and gave Cameron a rapid-fire rendition of what he had just learned.

When he was through briefing Cameron, Peterson mused aloud, "I wish to hell I could figure out what phase two is supposed to be. I couldn't get a clue from anybody up there. This group is so damned compartmentalized, all these different categories of workers don't even know what the others are doing. 'Course that's helped me with my cover. They think I'm Willard Jensen, an FBI agent who got screwed over by a politician. Actually I guess you could say his wife got the screwing; she left him for a Congressman from his district. Anyway, nobody here even knows what Jensen looks like. They just know he was a chopper pilot in 'Nam like me. Meantime, I've got Jensen safely locked up in an 'undisclosed location'."

Cameron thought for a moment, and said, "You know, something's been bothering me. A minute ago you said the captain was a Level Four, which is supposed to be the highest category in this group. Presumably there's also a Level Four involved with phase two. Wouldn't somebody have to coordinate all these categories of people?"

"Whoa, good point. There must be a central planning committee that puts it all together. Maybe there is a fifth category of operative. I only wish I knew as much as they do right now."

"Maybe we know more than we think. I didn't get a chance to tell you that I overheard two crew members. They mentioned something about going back on land and tripping perimeter alarms at the nuclear plant. Do you suppose that will be a signal to someone inside?"

"Damnamighty! I knew it but it just didn't register. Tanya said that she and her crew have to do something at the nuclear facility. They may have similar plans all around the country, to take control of the power grid. Why sink the ship, though?"

"Maybe to create a diversion while they do whatever they have to do at the plant. Gene, we've got to find a way to warn them at the power plant. My Mary's on emergency duty, and there's no telling what they'll do to the control room crew."

"I understand what you're saying, but there's nothing we can do right now. I can't get up with Elliott, and we don't know who the group has stationed in the nuclear facility. Besides, we've got some business we have to take care of right here first. Remember, your friend Larry is on the bridge guiding us up river and they don't plan to let him leave alive. Plus there's enough explosive power on board to level most of Riverport, if the hurricane doesn't do it first. Oh yeah, and we've got two more crewmen wandering around. They could screw up any plans we make. I think we should wait until Tanya takes them ashore just past Riverport.

"So what do we do now?"

"Come with me. I've got to go down to the hold and get the chopper ready. We might just need it for ourselves. We'll find you a hiding place down there."

They left the room and Peterson led Cameron down a series of stairs and passageways to the ship's rearmost main hold. To Cameron, it appeared much like a cavernous car ferry, with lane-lines painted onto the metal decking for trucks to roll on board. There were a few vehicles scattered throughout, fastened securely against the increasing pitch and roll of the ship. Cameron whispered to Peterson, "Do you think the Captain forged a "hands off" order for the local Coast Guard? That would explain why there was no close inspection done."

Peterson replied, "Must have. He did say he was a desk jockey now, and I think he's been stationed at Coast Guard headquarters."

Soon the helicopter came into view. It had been lowered to the hold and was secured near the aft ramp. As they neared it, both men could hear water crashing against the rear of the ship. Listening to the ramp creak and moan as the ship rolled, Peterson remarked, "That worries me; I don't know how the ramp will hold up once the waters really get rough. Let's pray it stays together for this trip."

After directing Cameron to a hiding place behind two trucks, Peterson went back to get the helicopter flight-ready. When he finished the checklist he came back to give Cameron more directions. "Do you still have your communicator?" he whispered. When Cameron shook his head "no" Peterson fished one out of his pocket and handed it to him saying, "Lucky I have a spare. Heaven knows what you did with the first one. Just keep it on now. The only voice you should hear on it is mine, letting you know if I need you to come topside. If anybody finds you, shoot to kill because if you don't, I guarantee they'll take you down."

As Peterson finished his last admonition, both of them fell silent at the faint sound of someone approaching. They recognized the voices of Pegram and Roznik. Cameron ducked back into the shadows as Peterson sped back to the helicopter. When the two crewmen reached the helicopter, Peterson queried "What are you doing down here? Did you finish your jobs topside?"

Roznik answered, "Yeah, we're done. Cap'n wanted us to see if you needed any help. Weather's gettin' rougher and we gotta go, so he wants you back at the bridge."

"All right, thanks. I'm just about done here. Go ahead up and tell him I'll be right there."

The two men walked away and Peterson checked a few more things on the helicopter before going up. He shied away from Cameron's hiding place in case the two crewmen still lingered nearby.

Back on the bridge, Peterson could see occasional twinkling lights on the Riverport waterfront through the blowing rain as the ship went through the twists and turns of entering the river inlet. The town looked deserted and Peterson assumed most people had evacuated.

Before long, the last lights of the inhabited waterfront passed by on the port side.

The captain signaled for Peterson to take over guarding Larry and for Tanya to join Pegram and Roznik, who were readying the wooden motor launch to be lowered from the port bridge deck. Obedient to a fault, they prepared to lower the launch into the heaving waters below. The Captain slowed the ship to near idle speed, employing bow and stern thrusters to help maintain course. The two crew members and Tanya climbed aboard the launch, and Tanya set the gravity launch mechanism to lower them automatically to the water at a moderate speed.

As the launch dangled halfway between davit and water on its descent, a tremendous gust of wind and an unexpected swell hit the starboard side of the ship, setting off a disastrous chain of events for the launch's occupants.

The ship rolled hard to port, causing the launch to descend rapidly to a rising sea and hit the water hard enough to jar its occupants to the floor. As they lay momentarily dazed, the rolling motion stopped, the cables momentarily slackened and the launch floated for a fraction of a second on the crest of a swell. Before any of them could recover enough to unhook the cables, the ship abruptly righted itself. As a result, the cables whipped back, rotating the launch sideways, and slamming it and its occupants into the hard steel plating of the ship. The launch broke in half, and three lifeless bodies slipped out of it like rag dolls into the depths. The bow end of the launch followed them into the sea but the stern end, motor still attached, remained hooked to its cable.

The Captain, struggling to steady the ship, saw nothing of the port-side debacle. In the meantime, Larry and Peterson had been flung to the floor and Larry, still bound with the handcuffs, suffered several bumps and cuts on his head. Regardless, the captain ordered "Get the hell off the floor and give me some calls." Peterson told the Captain, "He can't guide you in if he hits the floor again. Why don't you unlock the handcuffs so he can steady himself?"

The Captain responded testily, "The keys went with Tanya, you hold him up." Steadying himself with one hand, Peterson did the best he could to help Larry off the floor and support him. The Captain had begun accelerating the ship as he steered it back on course, never confirming whether his co-conspirators made it to shore.

After a few minutes the lights of the munitions depot docks came into view on the port side. With no warning, the Captain veered the ship hard to port. Peterson shouted, "What the hell are you doing?"

The captain replied, "I'm ditching here, it's too rough to go any further. Go fire up the chopper."

Peterson shouted, "Are you crazy? If this ship blows up at the munitions terminal, there's no telling what could happen. At least get a little further up the river."

The Captain shouted back, "Who the hell are you to tell me what to do? Now go do what I told you."

Peterson had been waiting for Tanya and the others to leave before taking any action but he thought he would have more time to plan. Now he could wait no longer. Unholstering his pistol, he slammed its butt hard against the back of the Captain's head with his right hand as he shoved him away from the controls with his left hand. As the Captain hit the floor, Peterson quickly turned to the controls. He had been watching the Captain steer the ship, seeing enough to mimic his actions.

The ship was headed bow-first toward the loading platform. Impact would crush the bow and embed it into the pier. Even if the explosives on board did not detonate on impact, no one would be able to move the ship before the charges were set to go off on their own. With only seconds to go, Peterson spun the small steering wheel on the steering console hard to the right while pulling back on the throttle. Larry blurted out, "Don't pull back too hard on the throttle or we'll lose our steering momentum."

Peterson replied, "Got it. Now keep your fingers crossed because I can't even see the docks now."

Slowly, the Soprano lumbered to starboard. Peterson kept the wheel turned as far right as he could, easing the throttle back until Larry told him to stop. Peterson held his breath. It seemed like hours, but only seconds later he spied the pier just off the port bow. He was just about to breathe again when the entire ship suddenly jolted leftward, accompanied by a thunderous roar. Peterson was barely able to hold onto the console and remain standing but Larry was again tossed to the floor, landing beside the Captain.

"What the hell was that?" asked Peterson. He quickly scanned the deck, he added, "Doesn't look like any of our charges went off."

When no-one responded, Peterson turned and saw Larry on the floor. Larry was able to struggle upright and make his way to a seat attached to the floor near the console. Peterson inquired, "You all right? "

"Yeah, I think so. Our stern must have slammed into a piling at the end of the pier when we came about." Looking out over the deck below he added, "Looks like at least one of the cargo containers shifted when we hit but we can't do anything about that now."

Larry immediately began telling Peterson how to get the ship back on course. Once the steering was stabilized, Peterson grabbed Larry by the arm and rushed him outside. The wind whipped stinging rain against their faces as he guided Larry to the rail.

Again unholstering his pistol, Peterson shouted to Larry, "All right, hold your arms out as far as you can behind you and your hands as far apart as you could get them."

Still dazed from his earlier fall, Larry stared back at him for a few seconds.

Peterson said, "Come on, come on, we've got to get moving."

Larry did as he was told. Placing the gun-barrel squarely against the chain of the handcuffs, Peterson said, "I'm afraid our friend Tanya took the key with her," as he blasted the chain in two. "Back inside quick. It's up to you to get us the hell out of here. I hope you're up to it." Although still shaken, Larry nodded his head in affirmation.

Once back inside the bridge, Larry quickly took the helm and held the ship on course. He nodded toward the Captain on the floor and asked Peterson, "He still alive?" Peterson responded, "He is, but I don't want him in here with us.

Grabbing the Captain's wrist with one hand and balancing himself with the other, Peterson dragged him to the door and pushed it open. He had one foot almost out the door when a strong gust hit it, slamming it shut and nearly crushing his foot. Mumbling "Man that could have hurt", he dropped the Captain and grabbed some chart books from a nearby rack, wedging them in the doorway.

Peterson grabbed the Captain's wrist again and backed out the door, struggling to drag the dead weight a few steps to the outer rail. He used his own handcuffs to hastily chain the Captain's wrist to some pipes that ran parallel to the rail, then he jumped back through the door. Seeing Larry's questioning look as he stumbled back into the bridge, Peterson said, "After what they were planning to do with you, I wouldn't worry too much about his welfare."

Larry said, "I thought you were part of 'they'."

"So did your friend Cameron, when I found him out on deck."

"Cameron's here? Alive? The way I heard them talking earlier, I was afraid he'd been long gone. Oh hell, I should have known; lawyers and cockroaches, you can't get rid of either one."

Cocking one eyebrow, Peterson said, "I'm sure glad you two are friends."

Larry responded wryly, "Hell, he'd say something just as nice about me. But I know he'd have been just as worried about me for real. Where is he now?"

With a start, Peterson quickly retrieved another communicator from his pocket, saying, "I just about forgot; he'd probably like to know what's going on. While I talk to him, can you turn this thing around?"

"Sure can. With the bow and stern thrusters on this baby I can just about turn on a dime. 'Course with this wind it might be more like a quarter." With that, Larry began maneuvering the ship into a one hundred eighty degree turn back down river and said, "What's next?"

"We're going to get as far away from land as we can."

"You're kidding. You do remember there's a hurricane about on top of us?"

"You heard everything that's been said here. We can't risk grounding anywhere along the waterfront. When those charges go off it's going to be an inferno. By the time the wind spreads the flames around, the fire alone could level what the hurricane doesn't. Set your course downriver and see if you can get some weather information. And clean up your face." He fished a handkerchief from his pocket and tossed it to Larry. On wiping his face and seeing the red residue on the handkerchief, Larry turned to Peterson and said, "Damn, son, why didn't you tell me how banged up I was?"

Peterson responded, "Well I meant to in my spare time, but you know...."

As Larry turned the ship down river, Peterson put on the communicator and called to Cameron, telling him "The coast is clear, you need to come up to the bridge."

Cameron said, "It sounded like we hit the coast. What's been going on?"

"Tell you when you get up here. Come on up, fast." After giving Cameron directions to the bridge, he added, "Just before you take that second stairway I mentioned, you'll see a set of lockers. They've got foul-weather gear in them. Put one outfit on and bring two more with you." He cut the communicator off before Cameron could ask who the second set of rain gear was for. Cameron assumed it was for the ship's captain and hurried to get to the bridge.

The last approach to the bridge was outside. Clutching the rain gear in front of him with one hand, Cameron crouched low and grabbed what he could to steady himself as he made halting progress down the narrow passage. From past experience with hurricanes, he estimated the speed of steady winds at fifty miles per hour, with gusts over seventy. Not even category one strength yet. Rain was intermittent, none coming down one moment, torrents coming down the next. When the rain came with a heavy gust, it hit his face like a wide-open fire hose. He could barely keep his footing as the ship bobbed and weaved through the waves.

When he was only fifty feet or so from the door, Cameron saw something laying on the deck and thought, *"Now I'm hallucinating; that looks like a person."* Just then the rain let up and he wiped his eyes. It was a person, a man handcuffed to a pipe, and he was holding a pistol against the handcuff chain. In that same second the man saw Cameron approaching. Too late, Cameron realized that the gun now was pointed his direction. As he skidded to a halt, a flash erupted from its muzzle.

CHAPTER THIRTY-THREE

When he heard the gunshot, Peterson charged outside with his gun drawn, swinging the door out so hard it slammed into the Captain's raised hand. A bewildered look crossed the Captain's face for a moment as his weapon, turned when hit by the door, fired its second shot of the evening straight through his head.

At the sound of the shot Peterson instinctively moved into a firing posture but quickly realized the Captain no longer posed a threat. For a few seconds, all he could do was stare in disbelief. Quickly regaining his composure, Peterson unlocked the handcuffs from the rail and shoved the Captain's body forward of the doorway. He tried to raise Cameron on the communicator, but got no response. Fearing the worst, he turned to look down the passageway and saw Cameron sprawled on his back, still clutching the rain gear. A small halo of red stained the deck below the back of Cameron's head.

Paterson had to crouch so low he was almost crawling as he scrambled to the motionless body and placed two fingers on Cameron's wrist to feel for a pulse. He felt the thump-thumping of a strong heartbeat. After a quick examination, he determined that Cameron had only a superficial wound on the back of his head.

Suddenly, a ferocious gust of wind rocked Peterson off his feet, and the air grew still. Wasting no time, Peterson scrambled to his feet and took advantage of the momentary lull to drag Cameron back to the bridge.

The strain of pulling Cameron's dead-weight so soon after dealing with the Captain's body left Peterson exhausted. As soon as he got Cameron inside, Peterson left him in a heap on the floor.

Peterson leaned back against the door, slid down to a sitting position, and tried to catch his breath. Larry stole some worried glances at Cameron's motionless form, but had to concentrate on the helm.

Before long, Cameron groaned, blinked his eyes open, and squinted at the room around him. Larry heard the groan and when he turned and saw Cameron staring at him, he said, "Nice of you to come visit, buddy."

Cameron replied, "Somebody told me you were out here goofin' off. Had to come see for myself." He sat up, still groggy.

Peterson, who was more rested now, said, "I thought he got you."

"He who?"

"He, the Captain of the ship. He's a Level Four and I put him out there to keep him out of the way. I could kick myself for letting him keep his weapon. With so much going on, I forgot he had it."

Cameron said, "I could kick you too, but under the circumstances I'll let it ride. I remember what happened now; when I saw that gun start to point at me, I stopped so fast my feet slipped out from under me. I recall hearing the gunshot as my head crashed into the deck and the next I knew, here I am. Guess the shot went over my head."

With a few grunts and groans, Cameron pulled himself up and stretched his back a few times. "No permanent harm done I guess," he said. He looked at Larry and asked, "What the hell happened to you? Your face is a mess." Larry responded, "I got clumsy kinda' like you did; only I went face-first. By the way, you oughta' see the back of your noggin. Bet you'll have a hell of a headache later."

Cameron reached behind and touched the back of his head, immediately saying, "Ouch". On seeing the blood on his hand, he looked around for a first-aid kit, finding one on the back wall. Before tending to his own head, he did the best he could to bandage Larry's wounds. By then, Peterson was standing again and he cleaned and dressed the cut on the back of Cameron's head, telling him, "Looks OK, not very deep. I'm sorry, I just forgot he had a gun."

Peterson continued to apologize profusely to Cameron, saying, "I can't believe I led you right into that. I'm getting too old and careless for this job. I should have at least cuffed both his hands around the rail." Cameron waved it off, saying, "Hey, we're not exactly under ideal conditions here. I'm just glad to see both of you still alive." Peterson and Larry both responded, "Likewise".

By now, the ship was nearing the river inlet. Peterson said, "Listen, I'm going to try and contact somebody," as he headed into the small radio room at the back of the bridge. Cameron stood in the doorway watching. None of the equipment worked. "Evidently the Captain never had any intention of reporting anything to anybody," he said. Every piece of the equipment has been disabled. Larry, is anything out there working?"

Larry tried the radio equipment at the console, but the only thing working was was a receiver for weather reports. The news was not good. Hurricane Mary had picked up considerable forward momentum, and the eye was expected to make landfall at Riverport within hours.

Larry looked at Peterson and asked, "What now, Cap'n?"

Peterson sighed loudly, and replied, "Keep heading for open water, as far from land as we can go in the time we've got. We only have a few hours before we go up like a volcano. Cameron, I forgot you don't know the whole story yet. Those containers on deck are packed with explosives that are set to go off at six in the morning."

Cameron said, "Explosives! Isn't there any way to defuse them?"

"No, the containers are locked and the keys went ashore with the two goons you saw near the helicopter. We wouldn't have time to defuse them all in the best of weather, and it'll only take one to set the rest off."

Cameron asked, "Are we all that's left on board?"

Peterson replied, "We're it."

They all fell silent, contemplating ways to avoid the unavoidable. Finally, Larry said, "There's no way we can outrun the storm. I think we need to run into it. Don't gape at me like that, Cameron. Look, the radar's still working. We can track the hurricane and run to its southeast side so the wind'll be behind us. If this ship holds together long enough, we can cut across to the eye, where there's no wind. Once we're there we can drop a launch. We'd still have some hellacious seas to deal with, though."

Cameron said, "I've got a better idea. Gene here knows how to fly a 'copter, and there's one below deck. He can get us back on land a lot faster with it, and we won't have to buck the waves."

Peterson shook his head as he spoke, "The air in the eye will be calm but the water won't. We'll be bobbing all over the place. How the hell do you expect me to fly out of that hold?"

Larry grinned as he answered, "Cap'n, you're about to find out what it's like to thread a needle in a moving car on a bumpy road. As soon as we get in the clear, well drop the aft ramp. You gotta' have that 'copter fired up and ready to fly out the ass end of this ship as soon as it drops. 'Course that's if we ever get that far."

While he talked, Larry steered the ship out of the inlet and into open waters. Already, the seas were beginning to break over the bow as he struggled to keep the vessel on course. According to the ship's instruments, winds were already at a steady seventy miles per hour.

On the weather radio, the reporter stated, "highest wind speeds around the eyewall have been clocked at one hundred fifty seven miles per hour; a category five storm. Hurricane Mary's forward speed is approximately fifty miles per hour, and the eyewall is about a hundred miles offshore."

"That gives us around two hours if we stand still," said Larry. "It'll be less if we're moving into it. If we're really lucky, she'll lose some punch now that the outer bands are hitting land."

Cameron thought about his promise to Mary that he would leave town if the hurricane reached category three or more. *"Well,"* he thought, *"I've left town alright. I'm glad she thinks I'm in a safe place."*

The sound of howling winds and driving rain outside drowned out nearly all other noises, but something permeated the din; an intermittent banging on the port side. Cameron and Peterson squinted through the sheets of rain, looking for the source of the noise. Finally, Peterson noticed that the cables were still hanging from the port motor-launch davit, and occasional gusts of wind would swing the cables away from the ship. When they swung back toward the ship, the banging could be heard.

"That's too loud to be nothing but cable hardware," said Larry. As he finished, a strong gust whipped along the port side, swinging the cable forward, and bringing the still-attached stern end of the launch into view just above the rail. In an instant it dropped out of sight, banging again on the side of the ship.

"Looks like Tanya and her friends didn't make it ashore after all," said Peterson.

Larry grinned broadly for a second and then turned serious, saying, "We've got to dump that debris before the wind blows it up here. After seeing what just happened, it wouldn't surprise me to see it come through these windows."

Peterson and Cameron looked at each other, knowing what they had to do. Cameron was still wearing the foul-weather gear. Peterson slipped his gear on and they both headed for the door. Before they opened it, Larry admonished, "find something you can use to tie yourselves off, otherwise you're gonna go flying."

Once they found some lengths of line in a locker, they tied some of it around themselves, leaving enough to loop around the rail. As they headed toward the door, Peterson asked Cameron, "You got a pretty bad bump on the head a while ago, you sure you're up to this?" Cameron replied emphatically, "I'm fine. Let's go."

The ship was on a straight course, and Larry was able to leave the helm just long enough to man the door. During a slight lull in the wind, Cameron and Peterson rushed through the portside door and Larry pulled it shut behind them. They immediately sat on the deck and tied the loose ends of their lines to the rail, and then started inching their way to the lifeboat davit, practically crawling on the deck. The driving rain stung their faces as they moved and they were forced to stop and hold tight each time the seas broke over the bow. As high up as they were, some of the overwash still reached them.

For ten minutes they fought to travel the short distance to the boat hoist. When they reached it they discovered that the cable brake was on. Cameron reached out once to disengage it, but a sudden burst of wind flung him backwards. He and Peterson both hit the deck and held tight.

The broken hull of the launch swung up to the rail once again, slamming into it and showering debris around them. As the hull dropped, the wind eased enough for Cameron to reach the brake release lever. When he disengaged it, the launch's remains descended rapidly into the waiting waves. The resulting slack in the cable allowed the hook to work free of the debris, which sank out of sight. Within seconds, Cameron engaged the hoist lever to pull the cables back in and signaled Peterson to head back to the bridge.

Cameron and Peterson crawled back to the bridge and were nearly to the door when a wave slammed into the the ship's port side. Peterson had already let go of the rail to reach for the door and was swept away in the overwash. Cameron saw him tumble backwards and then lost sight of him in the foam of the breaking water.

Larry's warning had proved fruitful; Peterson's lifeline suddenly pulled taut. The problem was, it was taut because Peterson had been swept over the rail and was dangling in the air several feet below the

146

passageway. He was limp, hanging by the rope tied around his waist and swinging in the wind like a rag doll.

Cameron swiftly tied off the slack in his line. He grabbed Peterson's line and strained to pull him up. At first he made little headway, but soon after he heard sputtering and coughing, the weight became more bearable. Peterson had come to and was finding some footholds.

As both men strained to get Peterson over the rail, Cameron noticed that the wind had grown less severe, even though the noise was still deafening. He realized that the ship had turned so that its port side was temporarily leeward. Taking advantage of the break, both men scrambled to their feet, untied their lifelines, and rushed through the door, collapsing onto the floor once again.

When Larry turned to look at them, all he could see was a tangle of yellow rain gear sprawled in every direction. Cameron gasped, "I don't think I can take any more trips outside."

Although Larry was struggling with the helm to take a new course, he managed to fire out, "Nice of you boys to come back in from your little stroll. I finally got her turned enough to cut you some slack. Now we got another problem." Pointing toward the main deck and its containers, he said, "You might say we've got a loose cannon out there. One of the containers is wobblin'. When he saw their pleading stares, he added, "don't worry, you don't hafta' go back out. Ain't no way we can do anything about it now. Just keep your fingers crossed it don't break loose completely."

At the time, Cameron and Peterson were too exhausted for the possible outcome to register with them. Each of them stayed on the floor to rest.

CHAPTER THIRTY-FOUR

Before long, Peterson and Cameron regained their strength enough to stand with Larry near the helm and peer out over the deck below, holding onto whatever they could find to steady themselves. As the ship pitched and rolled, they could see that one of the containers was shifting somewhat obliquely, but seemed to be holding fast for the time being.

As he stared at the cargo below, Cameron had a chance to think about how much the ship was bobbing in the water. For the first time since boarding, he started to feel queasy. Evidently, Peterson felt the same way as he queried, "Any buckets or anything in the room? Up to now I haven't really noticed how much we're rolling here."

All Larry could offer was, "Just take some deep breaths and get that fan to blow on you. I ain't got time to play nurse."

A fan was attached to the console, and Peterson turned it so its breeze wafted by all their faces. Larry looked at the other two and laughed, "You two look a little less green. Just try to think about something else, like how in the hell are we going to get out of this alive."

Peterson was about to respond when a loud tone came from the weather radio. The hurricane report was being updated. "Hurricane Mary lost some intensity once the outer bands crossed land," the reporter said. "Winds in the eyewall have subsided to one hundred thirty miles per hour, but the direction and forward velocity remain the same, north-northeast at fifty miles per hour. The storm is on a fast track directly toward Riverport, North Carolina."

Larry had now brought the ship past the shoals and into open seas. He checked the radar, made some quick calculations, and told

Cameron and Peterson, "If we're gonna get a tailwind, we'll have to head southeast from here. The way the shoreline curves westward in these parts, we'll still be plenty far out."

Larry's face became a study in concentration, his eyes darting back and forth over the array of instruments and controls at the helm as he fought to keep the ship on course. Cameron and Peterson watched in silence. Every once in a while Larry would coax the ship on, as if speaking to a living person; "Come on, come on, go right, you can do it," or "Damn girl, I know you got more in you than that."

The roaring wind outside grew louder as they dove further into the maelstrom. It sounded as though a jet aircraft was trying to take off next to the bridge. Larry shouted, "Wind speed hasn't dropped below ninety-five knots in the last fifteen minutes and it's jumping to a hundred twenty-five here and there." To Peterson he said, "That's a steady hundred nine miles an hour with gusts up to a hundred forty-four, Cap'n. "

The Soprano bobbed like a child's plastic boat in a bathtub. It would ride up a mountain of water, hover at the crest, then plunge down into a trough, and each time Cameron felt it would keep going straight to the bottom of the sea. With the torrent of rain and sea water washing over the windows, he wondered if he wasn't already there. Other times the ship rolled precariously close to capsizing when waves crashed into its side. Cameron thought, *"I'll never find a roller coaster to top this. Then again, I'm not going to live long enough to find another roller coaster anyway."*

Larry kept steering on instruments and instinct, constantly adjusting the controls. At one point he shouted out, "We got the wind at our backs now, we might get all the way up to seven knots." Looking at the radar screen, he added, "If we can hold together, looks like we're about a half hour away from the eye."

Seeing that his wristwatch read ten minutes to five, Cameron shouted, "We've got an hour and ten minutes 'til we blow sky high, so no problem. Take your time."

Larry retorted with a grin, "Why don't you write a legal brief while you're waiting, lawyer boy. That'll get us there faster."

Peterson said, "I can't believe you two are still raggin' each other at a time like this."

Larry responded, "It's the only way we can keep from losin' it." Cameron nodded his head in agreement.

As Larry finished speaking, the bow broke through a wave and they all jumped as a loud crash resounded from the deck below. As he tried to peer through sheets of falling water, Larry said, "That didn't sound good, but I can't see a damn thing out there." He fell silent again, his concentration focused on getting to the eyewall.

As they drew closer to the eyewall, the roaring winds whipping through the rigging created a shrill chorus. During a brief pause in the rainfall they saw what had crashed on the deck; a container was lying upside down, about fifty feet from its original mooring. Cameron wondered aloud, "I can't believe the impact didn't cause it to blow. I guess that one must be empty."

Then, without warning, the entire ship trembled as a gigantic wave broke over the starboard bow. The rushing water found its way under the loose container, and water and wind lifted it as if it were a child's toy box, hurling it several hundred yards into a waiting wall of water. On impact, the container erupted into an inferno, instantly turning night to day. The heat emanating through the bridge windows felt like the mid-day sun and the noise reverberating against the metal walls was deafening. Within seconds, the explosive force was scattered by the raging storm and the ship was again enveloped in wind and darkness.

Larry let out a long, low whistle, and said nothing further. For a while no one uttered a word. At length, Cameron said shakily, "Well, so much for assumptions. The first trip across the deck must have loosened something that sparked when it hit the waves. Man, if that's what happens when just one of those containers goes up, I don't even want to think about them all going at once." Larry and Peterson remained silent.

For twenty more minutes they endured the onslaught in silence. Every few minutes, Cameron looked at his watch, his thoughts rambling; *"I've never had so many minutes seem like hours. How can I be bored and scared at the same time? It's past sunup and I can't even see the first glimmer of daylight. Are we there yet?"* He tried to think about model railroading, carpentry, his work, anything to distract him from the nightmare he was living. Finally he gave up. *"Odd,"* he thought, *"I should be scared to death or mad as hell or something, but suddenly I feel... nothing. Something somewhere in my brain has clicked into 'neutral' I guess."* As the next minutes ticked by, he simply stared out the window, automatically adjusting his grip and balance to the wild gyrations of the ship. At one point he stole a glance at Peterson, who was also staring out the window blankly.

Cameron jumped when Larry suddenly shouted, "The clouds ahead are a whole lot lighter and that jives with what the radar says. We're almost at the eyewall. Y'all boys go below now and get the helicopter ready. We won't have much time once we break through. When we get in the eye, I'll set a course then come down to join you. Go!"

Wasting no time, Cameron and Peterson scrambled back into their rain gear. They went out the starboard door since it was leeward of the wind but as soon as they got to the passageway, they hit the deck crawling. As the ship continued to pitch and roll, they hung on to pipes that ran the length of the passageway decking. At times they flopped around the deck like freshly caught fish but they held their grip and finally made it to a doorway. Peterson got on his knees, swung the door open, and rolled through it. Cameron followed right after and pulled the door shut. From there they were able to make better time down inside passages and stairways.

As they bounced and jostled their way through the ship, Cameron said, "We look like a couple of damn drunken sailors."

Peterson replied, "Drunk would be nice about now."

When they reached the main hold, Peterson stopped for a second and grabbed Cameron by the arm. "Ssh," he said, "listen." Cameron cocked his head. The roar of the wind had stopped. Cameron shouted, "We did it, we made it to the eye!" Peterson looked at his watch and said, "Don't get too excited, we've only got about fifteen minutes until those charges go off. I hope to hell Larry's right behind us." They took off running toward the helicopter.

Fortunately, all the cargo in the hold held tight against the rolling and bobbing of the ship. As Peterson jumped into the helicopter and started firing up the rotors, Cameron began uncoupling the clamps and hold-downs that secured the craft to the deck. Within moments, Larry appeared, running at top speed toward the aft ramp controls. As he rushed by them, he shouted, "We're in the sunshine, boys, but the eye's coming across fast and we're still bobbin' like a cork."

As Larry reached the control panel and engaged the ramp-lowering sequence, Peterson got the helicopter fully running. The 'whap, whap, whap' of the rotors in confined quarters was nearly as deafening as the winds had been.

Larry sped back to the waiting helicopter, ducking low to avoid the rotors, and clambered into the back seat. Cameron unclamped the last hold-down and jumped into the front passenger seat. They buckled themselves in for the ride as the ramp slowly descended to its horizontal loading position. Peterson was already wearing a headset with earphones and a microphone and motioned for Larry and Cameron to each wear a set. When they put them on, he said, "I don't want to lift off until the ramp gets all the way open. If I do, the deck might come up to meet us.

Larry adjusted the microphone on his headset and shouted, "I got the ship on automatic headed to the far eyewall and it won't take long to get there. As long as the seas stay about the same, she'll stay pretty much on course. Keep your fingers crossed boys."

Cameron grimaced for a second and replied, "That's good Larry but you don't have to shout now. In fact I'd rather you didn't; it's killing my ears."

In a normal voice, Larry responded, "Sorry buddy, I forgot," and slapped him on the back. For good measure, he slapped Peterson on the back and said, "All right Cap'n, I've done the hard part so far. It's your turn now."

As the ramp slowly descended, golden sunshine flooded into the hold. Cameron said, "I'll never complain about getting up at sunrise again," but the sudden glare momentarily blinded him. Squinting and looking toward the floor while his eyes adjusted, he heard Peterson on the earphones saying, "There's a pair of sunglasses at the left side of your seat. When Cameron found them in a pouch to his left and quickly flung the sunglasses onto his face, he could see that Peterson wore a similar pair.

As the ramp neared horizontal position, something besides sunshine began flooding in. A wave hit the ship and huge amounts of sea water poured through the opening, sloshing and foaming around the helicopter's landing skids. Peterson said, "We gotta go. Now!"

Timing himself to the now-regular movement of the swells, Peterson took in a deep breath and eased the stick back as the stern of the ship started up a crest.

His feet and hands moving in perfect rhythm, Peterson eased the helicopter through the opening. A landing skid sparked along the ramp and Peterson slightly overadjusted. When he did, the tail rotor barely nicked an upper beam and the helicopter began to wobble. Cameron held his breath as Peterson deftly brought the craft under control. It cleared the opening just as the Soprano topped the crest.

As they began to fly forward, Cameron turned and craned to see the ship. As it slid into the trough of the swell, a wave hit its stern obliquely, sending tons of ocean water into the the opening where they just had escaped.

Peterson rapidly ascended to distance the helicopter as much as he could from the floating bomb, checking his watch as he raced toward the forward eyewall. When they were about a quarter mile away, he abruptly turned the craft and hovered in place to view the receding vessel. By then it had taken on so much water that it was listing hard to starboard. Glancing at his watch, Peterson began counting down from ten. When he reached five, the ship rolled over completely. When he reached zero the tons of explosives, securely attached to the deck in watertight containers, detonated. Streaks of bright orange and yellow fanned across the sky, competing with the sun's golden rays. As far away as they were, Cameron felt the concussive force jolt the helicopter. In seconds, the High Sea Soprano was no more.

Larry said reverently, "She was a hell of a tough ship." and stared ahead for a few seconds, then he said to Peterson, "Reckon we'd better go while the gettin's good. Where to now, Cap'n?"

Spinning the craft back toward the receding eyewall, Peterson said, "I guess I can tell you boys now that I haven't flown one of these things in over twenty-five years." After the color drained from Cameron's face, he started to speak but Peterson interrupted, saying, "No, no time to gab, we've gotta get to the nuke plant. Larry, you're the navigator here, give me a clue on which way to go." Larry quickly calculated a route using navigation equipment on the helicopter and directed Peterson to head north northeast with the hurricane's eye. Peterson turned the chopper as directed and opened the throttle all the way. In the meantime, he switched on the onboard radio and began tuning. Cameron asked, "Who in the world are you trying to reach?"

Peterson replied, "I'm trying to get Elliott on the sheriff department's frequency. We still have a lot to do." He got the frequency he was looking for and he began calling "Bee, this is Butterfly" several times over, with nothing but static in return. Cameron said, "You know, the hurricane's right over them now. I imagine there's too much interference."

Peterson started to answer, "I know, but with our elevation I was hoping to..." but was interrupted by a voice on the loudspeaker.

Although the sound was scratchy, it was unmistakably Elliott saying, "Where the hell are you?"

Peterson replied, "In the air, in the sunshine, and headed your way. Diamond Jim and another 'guest' are with me. I don't have time to explain. Listen... "

Peterson was cut off by a tap on the shoulder from Cameron, so he told Elliott, "Stand by."

Cameron was waving the communicator he had just fished from his pocket and told Peterson, "Remember he's on the public airwaves. Try this. It might work from up here too."

Peterson quickly put the communicator on and said into the radio microphone, "Elliott, put your other ears on." Within seconds, he could hear Elliott in the communicator earphone saying, "Butterfly?"

Peterson told Elliott, "Good, we can have a private conversation now."

Elliott responded, laughing, "Put your ears on? You drivin' an eighteen wheeler out there?"

Peterson said, "Very funny Elliott. Listen, we're in a chopper in the eye of the hurricane. Don't ask questions, just tell me where you are."

"Right now, I'm in the emergency command center, wonderin' if the roof is gonna stay on. I'm on the sheriff's emergency response team coordinating communications. I'm sure as hell glad you're both safe."

"Thanks. Are you at the airport?"

"We were but when they started talkin' category five, the Sheriff moved us to the nuclear plant office complex. The buildings here are supposed to hold up to high winds better. Luckily once the hurricane got over land, it backed off to a category three."

"That's perfect. Look, I need you to do some things..." Elliott cut him off saying, "Hold on," and came back in a few seconds saying, "Had to get somebody to cover my post. I'm gettin' some strange looks."

"They'll just have to keep looking. Listen, you need to move fast; the eye is just about over you. I need clearance to land as close to the reactor containment building as possible and I need you to meet me so we can all go inside the building together. I also need you to bring a few things. Just get there the best way possible. Can you do that?"

"Getting the clearance as we speak. What do you need me to bring?"

Peterson enumerated the items he needed and signed off so he could concentrate on his flying. He said to Larry, "Are we still on the right track?"

Larry responded, "Best I can tell Cap'n. I can't see anything that's under the eyewall, but that looks like some of Riverport just ahead in the sunshine. Waterfront's pretty messed up from the storm surge, but it looks like the town's not too bad off. OK, there's our main street. Turn about twenty degrees northeast. We'll be there fast."

In a few minutes the huge blue structure that housed the reactors loomed into view as the eyewall passed over it. Peterson began his landing approach.

CHAPTER THIRTY-FIVE

Peterson bypassed the helicopter pad, which was too far from the reactor building. In the middle of some wind-blown debris near a side entrance to the building, he spied a clearing that looked large enough to land in and he headed for it. As he approached to land, Peterson radioed Elliott where to meet them.

After clearing the landing with plant security and gathering the items Peterson had asked him to bring, Elliott bolted from the command center. Clothed in bulky rain gear with arms loaded, it took him a few minutes to pick his way through tree branches and other debris to reach his companions, who were just climbing from the helicopter as he arrived. He said, "Good to see ya, come on," and ran ahead of them to the entry stairs leading to the side door.

The sky was already growing dark and the wind was picking up, so they did not have time to secure the helicopter. Taking a quick look back at it Cameron thought, "I don't think we'll see that baby in one piece again."

Elliott had arranged for a plant security officer to open the solid metal door for them. The guard knew Larry and Cameron, but Peterson had to show his F.B.I. identification as they ran through the door into a hallway. Pointing to the cuts and bruises on Larry's head, Elliott told the guard, "Bobby, how about seeing that he gets medical attention. And see if you can get hold of Sandy and let her know he's safe. I know she's worried sick over him. We'll be all right."

The guard said, "Will do," and hurried off with Larry in tow. When he got out of earshot, Peterson said, "Now we just have to figure out where the control room is."

Elliott responded, "On the emergency response team we have to be ready for all kinds of crazy things, so we have to know our way around in here. Follow me."

Peterson said, "That's good Elliott, but first, we need to do a little planning. Looks like you brought everything we need. When we get to the control room, I'll go in first and you two guard the door until I give you the all clear." He continued outlining their plan of attack and then they got ready to move to the control room. He had to speak louder by the minute as the eyewall enveloped the building and the wind rapidly accelerated past a hundred miles per hour. Right before they headed down the hallway, they were startled by a loud bang as the wind flung something against the heavy metal door behind them.

Elliott led them through several corridors and up two flights of stairs to the control room. Outside the control room door, Peterson signaled Elliott and Cameron to stand on either side of the entryway and then drew his pistol. Elliott then entered code numbers into the keypad for the door lock. Bursting through the door, Peterson shouted, "F.B.I., nobody move!" Everyone in the control room froze in mid-operation, some with hands hovering over controls. He continued, "All right, finish what you have to do but keep your hands where I can see them, and turn my direction with your hands up when you finish." Two turned immediately, including Mary Scott, and the rest quickly followed. As each person turned, Peterson aimed his gun at them until he could see they held no weapons.

After the last person turned, Peterson called for Elliott and Cameron. Guns drawn, they appeared in the doorway, surveying the room. Mary nearly fainted on sight of Cameron. She had assumed that he left town when the evacuation notice was given. She started to go to him, but the look he gave her and an almost imperceptible shake of his head made her stay put.

Peterson moved to a spot where he could view all the room's occupants and the doorway at the same time, nodded toward Larry and Elliott and said, "I want to thank you boys for getting me this far," as he pointed the gun in their direction. Laughing, he said, "Cameron, you told me the next time I pointed this thing at you I had to fire it, so...." And he fired. Two shots in rapid succession.

Neither Cameron nor Elliott had time to react. Shock and disbelief registered on their faces as a bullet hit each of them in the middle of the chest, jolting them out of the doorway into the hall beyond.

Most everyone in the room simply stared at the doorway in shock. Mary rushed past Peterson in a panic, screeching "You son of a bitch, what have you done?" as she disappeared into the hallway. Peterson started to follow her, pistol at the ready, but a female voice in the control room said, "Let her go."

Peterson spun to see the source of the command. It was one of the operators, who had just finished entering something on a keyboard. She appeared to be in her thirties, dark haired with sharp features. Peterson said, "I know you were waiting for our signal, but just about everything went wrong with our phase of the operation. First the Captain went nuts and tried to crash the munitions terminal. I know we need to keep the country's defenses intact against outsiders so I have no idea what he was trying to do. Then your messengers drowned in the storm."

She nodded her head but said nothing, so he continued, "By the time all that happened, the storm was too far along for us to reach our destination, and I had to get here to signal you." Pointing to the door, he continued, "My 'friends' out there helped me get here. I hope it's not too late for you to carry out your mission."

She stared at him for a few seconds before answering, and finally said, "I'm Betsy, Level Four. I think there'll be some disappointment in the central committee, but under the circumstances, you'll probably be excused. I can still go on. The rest have been waiting for my signal to take command of their facilities. Our day has arrived."

Pointing to the rest of the control room personnel, Betsy continued, "We won't need these people. Dispose of them in any way you find convenient. I have to send out the command." She then turned to her computer keyboard and with a dramatic flourish, poised to strike a key, saying, "We are about to make hist…"

She was unable to finish her sentence. With snake-like speed, Peterson grabbed her wrist and whipped her and her chair several feet from the keyboard. Aiming his pistol at her temple he said, "Don't even move a hair," and took a few steps away from her.

As Peterson finished speaking, Cameron and Elliott rushed through the still-open doorway with guns drawn and aimed at the rogue operator. Mary appeared in the doorway behind them, looking pale and shaken. Peterson glanced briefly enough to see her and said, "Sorry about the fright, Gravy Boat, but it was the only way we could flush this Level Four operative. Your husband will probably have a nasty bruise behind that Kevlar. I wasn't sure which shock would be harder on you; seeing him shot or seeing him come back to life. Now Miss Betsy, we need to talk about your friends…"

His sentence was punctuated by an explosive sound, followed by the thud of Betsy's body as it hit the floor. As a stream of crimson flowed across the floor from Betsy's side, Peterson spun around to the source of the sound. A second operator, still seated, was holding a smoking, single-shot Derringer, smiling. Peterson quickly turned his pistol on him and the man casually dropped the derringer to the floor.

The man was slightly-built, also in his mid thirties, with light brown hair. Still smiling, he spoke in a southern drawl. "You idiots, you stupid American idiots. Your guns don't worry me. We're all gonna die together anyway."

Peterson, worried that the man might have wrapped himself in explosives, barked, "Keep your hands where I can see them." Pointing toward the other employees, he asked Mary, "How well do you know the rest of these folks?"

She replied, "I've been working with all of them for several years and know them well."

Peterson told them, "All of you get out and go as far from this room as you can. Go! Mary, you stay here with us." As Elliott helped the employees quickly file out of the room, Cameron and Peterson kept aim on the man. When the last of them was gone, Elliott closed and locked the door.

Peterson gave the man a quick pat-down and found no other weapons or explosives on him. Cameron then turned to the man and asked, "All right now, what the hell are you doing here and who the hell are you?"

The man answered, immediately losing some of the drawl; "I- no, my fellow soldiers and I- want your country to stop interfering with our part of the world. After today, you will be too distracted with your own troubles to bother with anyone else. With luck, your government will collapse when your people see the disasters we've spawned. We've had sleeper cells all over your country for years, waiting for our chance. You've seen our work in a few experimental unexplained 'accidents' here and there. You saw one of our larger experiments in New York and at the Pentagon a few years ago."

Peterson slammed his fist on a table next to him and exclaimed, "Damn! How could I have been so stupid. I should have seen the connection."

Sneering at Peterson, the man said, "It was our plan that nobody would see the connection. We have blended with you people and gained your trust, but we have never lost sight of our mission. Your foolish bureaucrats gave us just the organization we needed. The founders of the group were weak scholars, not leaders. They called themselves the 'Hornet's Nest'."

Cameron said, "Cute," and after a questioning look from Peterson added, "That's what the British called Charlotte, North Carolina, during the American Revolution. It was a hotbed of patriotic idealism."

The man snorted and said, "Whatever. We quickly eliminated the organizers and their stupid name, and found that we could easily manipulate some of your people's dissatisfaction with your government to our advantage. We found it amazingly easy to convince them that they are the true patriots who are saving you from yourselves." Pointing to the body on the floor, he said, "Even this stupid one here had no idea who I am; she thought she was doing her patriotic duty." He then let out a self-satisfied peal of laughter.

The man continued, "You see a fair-haired southern boy before you, but isn't it amazing what a little plastic surgery and hair bleach can do? In my sleeper cell, it was my job to study nuclear power plant technology and operations With some manufactured credentials, I was able to get a job at a Tennessee power plant. It was my good fortune to be available when an operator job came open at this facility, and we have built our grand plan around my presence here."

Peterson asked, "Why are you telling us all this. Aren't you afraid we'll undo your plans?"

The man arrogantly explained, "No, no, no, my friend, it's too late for that. You see, for several days I've been setting up a sequence of commands that will override all of the so-called 'fail-safe' systems that were built into this facility. While everyone was distracted by the storm, it was the perfect time for me to start my override program. While you were concentrating on the girl, Betsy, I was able to finish the sequence and we have only to wait a little while before we all gloriously melt into the earth along with this facility. I will go to my reward and you will take your place in hell. I've disabled the alarm system, so no one will even know what's happening until it's too late."

Stepping toward the man, Mary began to speak. "But..."

"Shut up woman," screamed the man. "I do not have to tolerate the insolence of you American women any longer." His cool ease had turned to livid anger. Cameron started moving toward the man, but Peterson waved him away and said to the terrorist through clenched teeth, "You may be able to do what you planned here, but you won't get close enough to Betsy's keyboard to send out the word to your buddies."

The man responded, "I need do nothing more. When word of this meltdown reaches the airwaves, my fellow soldiers will know our time has come, and they will unleash events that you cannot even imagine. It will be a long time before your country recovers, if ever." A self-satisfied smirk crossed the man's face.

"The hurricane set back our little plan to get things started," he continued. "We were going to explode our charges next to a loaded munitions ship at the terminal. Unfortunately, the munitions ship was taken out to sea to avoid the storm a few days ago. You see my friend, the Captain knew his orders were to head for the munitions terminal dock all along. He still could have crippled your ability to ship weapons from here, even if my phase of the plan didn't work. I don't know how you foiled those plans, but no matter. We'll make a much more spectacular statement right here because my phase of the plan is working."

Looking at his watch, the man smugly said, "I will say my goodbyes to you all, and you might wish to pray to your God for your souls, because we will all be leaving soon. I know I am going to a great reward."

For a few seconds, all that could be heard was the roar of the wind outside. Cameron, Peterson and Elliott looked at the floor dejectedly. Cameron reached for Mary, wanting her close for their final minutes.

But suddenly, Mary strode over to the man and gave him a sound backhand across his face. He started to rise out of his chair toward her but she slammed her fist down on the top of his head so hard that he abruptly sat back down, momentarily dazed. Peterson, Cameron and Elliott were also momentarily stunned at this outburst from Mary. Although Cameron had evoked some wrath from her from time to time as husbands are wont to do, he had never seen her quite so furious. They continued to keep their weapons trained on the man, in spite of the surprise from Mary.

Mary then leaned in toward the man and said, "Look you smug little asshole, you tell me to shut up one more time and you're going to be missing a little something you'll need for all those virgins you think you're going to go terrorize in the afterlife. I've always thought there was something funky about you and your companion that you so sweetly dispatched over there."

Taking a moment to regain her composure, Mary stood over the man and continued in low tones, "Ever since you and Betsy started here, something never seemed quite right, and after my husband here told me I needed to start watching things, I really kept my eye on you. With your little attitude about women I'm sure you figured I'd be too dumb to figure anything out, so you were actually easier to watch. Your problem is, you learned to talk the talk here, but you never learned to walk the walk. You didn't mingle with anyone at the plant, and I suspect you pretty well kept to yourself outside." The man glanced at his wristwatch, appearing a little less smug.

Moving away from him, she continued, "I'll grant that somebody taught you a fair southern accent, but you never spent enough time with real southerners to learn our culture. I can't even begin to list the things you've been clueless about when you ever did condescend to talk to any of your coworkers."

The man alternated between glaring contemptuously at Mary and glancing nervously at his watch. She moved closer to him and said, in very even tones, "The only meltdown around here is going to be yours, Bubba, because I've got you covered. When I got the alert, I started watching the system for any wrong moves on the controls. You gave yourself away when you punched the first wrong button after that. Everything you've done since then has been rerouted to cyberspace. Same for your dead patsy over there."

If eyes could shoot fire, Mary would have been burned through. The man knew she was right because the meltdown had not started yet. Nothing had changed. Without warning he bolted from the chair and ran for the door, knocking Mary to the floor on the way. Elliott fired one shot and missed but the man was out of sight too quickly for anyone to shoot again.

Peterson yelled for Elliott to guard the dead woman's computer and signaled Cameron to help him chase the fleeing man. Mary waved Cameron on, saying, "I'm fine, get him." Cameron and Peterson ran through the door and looked down the hall. They barely saw the man's heels as he turned right at another hallway. "He's got to be headed for the exit," shouted Peterson, "pick it up."

162

Each time they caught sight of the man, he was turning another corner. He made his way down both flights of stairs, still keeping his lead. At the bottom of the stairs, he could only go left. At the end of the hall was the entry door Cameron and Peterson had used earlier. As they burst through the door at he bottom of the stairwell, the man was leaning into the door with all his might, pushing it against the roaring wind.

The man had nowhere else to go. Cameron and Peterson both took aim and started walking toward the man. He looked back at them but kept pushing at the door. Peterson shouted, "Put your hands up, now!" Just then, the door swung open. Immediately the wind slammed it against the outer wall.

The man dove for the stair rail to brace himself as the wind burst through the door and down the hallway, knocking Cameron and Peterson to the floor. Although Peterson was momentarily stunned, Cameron stayed on the floor and kept crawling toward the doorway. He could see the man holding the rail, nearly being lifted off his feet by the howling fury.

Cameron crawled closer and took aim at the man but the winds suddenly subsided enough for the man to crouch and begin running down the stairs. Just as suddenly, a violent gust blew him upright. At the same time, part of the tail rotor from the now-shattered helicopter came whirling through the air like a boomerang. The look of shock and awe on the man's face as the rotor separated his head from his body was one that Cameron would never forget. The winds swiftly swept the lifeless body over the stair rail to the pavement below.

Astonished as he was at the turn of events, Cameron still had to close the door against the storm. He struggled down the hall, rolling and ducking to avoid bits of debris that hurtled at him through the open portal. When he finally reached the doorway, the wind abated long enough for him to step out and pull the heavy metal door shut. He ran back to Peterson, who was sitting up rubbing his head. Cameron asked, "Did you see what happened?"

Peterson answered, "Yup. Not quite the 'reward' he expected, I guess."

Cameron nodded silent agreement.

EPILOGUE

CHRISTMAS EVE

Cameron and Mary sat on the porch, drinks in hand, admiring the sunset over the waterway. The remains of an early supper lay on plates nearby. As sometimes happened in Riverport, December was mild with temperatures in the low sixties, so they decided to spend a quiet Christmas at the cabin.

The sunset was brilliant, fanning orange and red streaks across the deep blue sky. Well fed and relaxed, Cameron settled into his chair and rocked, idly taking in the spectacular sight before him. He felt something bump his arm and realized it was Mary, who said, "Wake up. If you start napping now you'll never get to sleep tonight." He rubbed his eyes and stood, saying, "I'm going to stroll down to the dock for a bit. Want to come?"

She said, "You go ahead. I'm going to finish watching the sun set."

As Cameron meandered down the wide sloping yard, memories flooded his mind. He and Mary had worked long hours removing limbs and leaves from the yards at home and at the cabin, and he now thought, "*I hate to imagine what might have happened around here if Hurricane Mary had stayed a category five. Then again, the hurricane would have been the least of our worries if the terrorists had succeeded.*"

When he spotted a small crease in the ground where he had dragged the canoe in his desperate attempt to get to the ship, Cameron thought, "*I must have been out of my mind. No sane person would have tried that. Ah, nobody ever said I was sane anyway.*"

On reaching the foot of the hill, Cameron strolled out on the new dock he finished a few weeks ago, replacing the one washed away by Hurricane Mary. There cradled on a rack was his green canoe. Someone had found it in a tree behind a second-row beach house and, seeing Cameron's name etched into one of the thwarts, had returned it to him. Looking at it he thought, "*I wish you could tell me what you went through to end up in that tree. I should write the company that made you and tell them they have one tough product.*" He admired the new artwork on the canoe. On each side he had painted the words "Green Hornet" in gold.

Looking at the tranquil scene as water gently lapped against the dock's pilings, Cameron shook his head, shuddering to think of what might have been. A few weeks after the incident at the nuclear plant, Peterson came to the Scotts' house to catch them up on what happened. He said, "We got enough information from Betsy's computer and the cell phone we found on the male terrorist's body for my agents to catch most of them. Some of them surrendered and some went down fighting, but hardly any got to carry out their objectives. Only two partially succeeded but they didn't do much harm. The scary thing is that they were positioned in nuclear plants, oil production facilities, hydroelectric dams, munitions plants, and lots of other strategic targets all over the country."

Mary said, "So all of the other operatives were waiting for word of the takeover in Riverport before they could start?"

Peterson replied, "That's right. In each location a Level Four thought he or she would take command of the facility. They had no idea another Level of terrorist was there to destroy it."

Cameron interjected, "Kind of a fifth and final category of terrorist."

"Yup. The idea was for the home-grown organization to take blame for the destruction, making people afraid to trust anybody in government. They figured that would start civil strife in addition to the devastation."

Cameron said, "Guess their perfect plan didn't factor us into it."

"Not by any stretch of the imagination could they have factored you two into their equation," replied Peterson, laughing.

Mary asked Peterson, "So what case do you go to next?"

Peterson replied, "This boy's getting out of government work. Well, for the most part. The President, you remember my distant cousin the President, wants me to take a top position in Homeland Security. I tell him I'm getting too old for all this, I'm ready to retire. So he makes me promise I'll be on call for special assignments and I say OK, as long as they're few and far between."

Cameron said, "Well, you be sure and keep in touch."

"I will, once I get back from a long vacation. By the way, you'll be interested to know that I pulled a few strings to get Elliott promoted to detective. He tells me he's going to take some night classes at the community college to get college transfer credits. I hear your friend Larry did fine."

"He did," Cameron answered. "He just had some superficial cuts and bruises. I told him it couldn't make him look any uglier anyway."

Peterson shook his head and laughed, saying, "You two don't give it up for anything do you?"

"Nope. But he still knows I was worried about him."

As he was leaving, Peterson asked Cameron to come outside with him to look at something. They walked to the end of the driveway where Peterson pointed to a new Dodge Ram parked across the street. Behind it was a government-issue sedan with a government-issue driver in a bad suit. Cameron said, "Now that's what you need to be driving. What happened to the other truck you had?"

Peterson replied, "That was just a rental. You like this one?"

Cameron answered, "Very nice." Eying the sedan, he added, "Did you really need an escort just to come see us?"

Smiling broadly, Peterson shook Cameron's hand and handed him the keys to the truck saying, "He's not my escort, he's my driver. I needed a way back to the airport. There's an envelope on the front seat. Oh, and here's my new cell-phone number." After handing him a slip of paper with the number on it, he gave Cameron a friendly whack on the shoulder and got into the sedan. Before he rode away he said, "I'm told the color on this truck is 'Patriot' blue. Oh and by the way, it has a factory-installed remote ignition."

For a few moments Cameron was too stunned to move. When he could move, he jumped straight into the truck and sniffed the the new-vehicle smell. He spied a plain envelope lying on the passenger seat, which he picked up and opened. Inside was a single-page handwritten letter, embossed with the Presidential seal. It read:

Gene Peterson has briefed me on the vital role you and your wife played in saving us from disaster, and also told me that you want no public acknowledgment, which I respect and will honor. However, I must tell you on my behalf and on behalf of the American people that we cannot thank you both enough for what you have done.

Gene also informed me that you have suffered a loss of transportation out of all this, so please at least accept this replacement as a personal gift from me, a small token of my gratitude. My wife and I would also like you both to join us at Camp David for Thanksgiving dinner. Please let Agent Peterson know if you accept, and arrangements will be made.

With warmest personal regards and thanks,

Frank Mills

The dinner was private and unofficial, the day before Thanksgiving. The only other guests were Larry and Sandy Gullege, Elliott Grainger and his wife, and Gene Peterson. By the time they finished their pumpkin pie, the President had been fully briefed on the entire episode. He took special interest in hearing how they flushed out the Level Four in the control room; giving the impression that Peterson was in league with the group after he "eliminated" Elliott and Cameron. The bulletproof vests supplied by Elliott were well hidden under bulky rain gear.

As serious as the whole adventure had been, the President could not stop laughing at the image of Mary hammering the Level Five terrorist on the head with her fist. He also delighted in hearing her tell about the various aspects of Southern culture that the man had been unable to understand and absorb.

~~

The sun was nearly all the way down by the time Cameron finished his reminiscences and he felt a bit chilled standing by the water. He turned and walked briskly up the hill. Mary was sitting where he had left her but he noticed she had gone inside and fixed each of them a fresh drink. He sat beside her and as they sipped their drinks she said, "I figured you were sorting out everything that's happened so I left you alone."

Cameron sighed and said, "I'm glad I got my name off the criminal appointment list. I don't think I could take any more clients like ol' Fishbait. It'll be nice doing the quieter stuff like real estate, wills and probate, and whatnot."

As the last glimmer of sunlight faded, Mary said, "You know, it's nice to have things humming along the way they should be. The bureaucrats are running things as always, the politicians are figuring out ways to complicate our lives, and we're all grumbling as usual. But there's nothing like having that freedom to bitch."

Cameron gave an enthusiastic "Here's to bitching" and held out his glass towards hers. She turned and tapped her glass on his. Giving her glass one more tap, he added, "And here's a Christmas toast to peace on earth; may we really see it in our lifetime." After a few moments gazing into each others' eyes, they retired into the cabin, quietly closed the door behind them, and turned out the lights.

THE END

CPSIA information can be obtained at www.ICGtesting.com

231156LV00001B/21/P